Sive

# Sive

*A Play in Two Acts*

## JOHN B. KEANE

**WITH INTRODUCTION AND COMMENTARY BY**
**JOANNA KEANE O'FLYNN**

MERCIER PRESS
IRISH PUBLISHER – IRISH STORY

MERCIER PRESS
Cork
www.mercierpress.ie


Original three act version first published 1959
This two act version first published 1986


© John B. Keane Occasions, 2009
© Notes and Introduction: Joanna Keane O'Flynn, 2009

ISBN: 978 1 85635 651 0

15 14 13 12 11

A CIP record for this title is available from the British Library

Printed and bound in the EU.

# CONTENTS

# CHARACTERS

| | |
|---|---|
| NANNA GLAVIN | An old woman (mother of Mike Glavin and grandmother of Sive) |
| MENA GLAVIN | Mike Glavin's wife |
| SIVE | The illegitimate granddaughter of Nanna Glavin |
| THOMASHEEN SEÁN RUA | A matchmaker |
| MIKE GLAVIN | The man of the house (husband of Mena Glavin, son of Nanna Glavin) |
| LIAM SCUAB | A carpenter, Sive's sweetheart |
| SEÁN DÓTA | An old farmer, suitor for the hand of Sive |
| PATS BOCOCK | A travelling tinker-man |
| CARTHALAWN | His musical son |

The action of the play takes place in the kitchen of Glavin's small farmhouse in a remote mountainy part of southern Ireland.

# INTRODUCTION

My parents, John B. Keane and Mary O'Connor married on 5 January 1955. They bought 'The Greyhound Bar' on 37 William Street, Listowel in the same year. One afternoon, while my father was working behind the counter, a haggard old man called in for a drink. He announced to all and sundry that a match had been arranged for him and that he would be getting married in the not too distant future. He requested that my unsuspecting father accompany him to a nearby jewellery shop to help him purchase a ring for his intended bride to be. My father visited the shop with the old man and thought no more about the encounter until months later. To his dismay, he heard from a friend that the aged man had married a girl who was too young for him. He also discovered that the young girl was deeply unhappy and ended up institutionalised after a nervous breakdown. This experience troubled my father for a long time after. The unfortunate girl's painful experience provided him with the material to write *Sive*.

My father had been experimenting with words since he was twelve. He had moderate success with articles published in *The Evening Press* and *Ireland's Own* and a radio play produced on RTÉ Radio. However, having attended Listowel Drama Group's award-winning production of *All Souls Night* by Joseph Tomelty with my mother in Listowel, John B. was stimulated to write *Sive*. 'When I came home that night I was impatient and full of ideas. I sent Mary to bed and filled a pint. I sat by the fire for a while and after a quarter of an hour I reached for my copy-book and pencil. I started to write and six hours later, or precisely at 6.30 a.m., I had written the first scene of *Sive*' [*Self Portrait*, 1966]. Within two weeks he had written the first draft of *Sive* and after much revision and editing, he submitted it to The Abbey Theatre, but was disappointed to have the play returned by post five weeks later. Rejected by The

7

Abbey Theatre, Listowel Drama Group championed my father and premiered *Sive* on 2 February 1959 in Walsh's Ballroom, Listowel. The play went on to win the All-Ireland Amateur Drama Final in Athlone in 1959. In the same year, the Abbey Theatre invited Listowel Drama Group to perform *Sive* for one week, which they did to popular acclaim.

The popularity of *Sive* established John B. as a writer and gave him the appetite to write several plays, novels, short stories and poems.

'I am a kind of writer. Nobody knows what kind of writer I am least of all myself. My ambition is that people will say some time "He was a kind of writer. He said things a different way from others" [*Self Portrait*, 1966].'

The rapturous rat-a-tat-tat of his typewriter will stay with me forever.

JOANNA KEANE O'FLYNN

# ACT ONE

## SCENE 1

[*The kitchen is poorly furnished, with an open hearth on its left wall. A door leads to a bedroom at the left side of the hearth. On the wall facing the audience there is a small window, and a door leads to the yard at the front of the house.*

*A large dresser, filled with ware in its upper half, stands between the door and the window. The lower part has doors. A third door is in the right wall of the kitchen with a small working-table at one side. Overhead a mirror hangs. Under the table are two buckets and a basin. A 20-gallon creamery tank stands between the door and the table with a half-filled sack of meal and a half-sack of flour.*

*A larger table stands in the middle of the floor. There are six sugan chairs; two beside the table; two by the fire; the others on either side of the dresser.*

*In the hearth a black skillet hangs from a crane and a large black kettle rests in a corner. An enamel bucket of drinking water is on the table.*

*The time is the recent past, a late evening of a bitter March day.*

*An old woman bent forward with age, dressed in black, sits near the fire surreptitiously smoking a clay pipe, she is* NANNA GLAVIN, *mother of the man of the house. She holds the tongs, idly gathering the fire; with the other hand she conveys the pipe continuously between lap and mouth.*

*When she hears the door latch lifting the tongs falls in her haste to conceal the pipe. A great quantity of red petticoat, and long boots tied up to her shins, are revealed when she lifts her skirt to hide the pipe.*

*Her skirts are hardly in place again, when another woman enters. The newcomer is strong, well-proportioned, hard-featured, in her early forties: her hair raven-black tied sharply in a bun gives the front of her head the appearance of being in want of hair, or being in a coif. She is* MENA, *wife of the man of the house.*]

9

| Mena: | There's a smell of smoke! |
| Nanna: | [*Crossly:*] 'Tis the way you left the fire when you went out. |
| Mena: | Not turf smoke, oul' woman, tobacco smoke! |
| Nanna: | Tobacco smoke how are you? [NANNA *seizes the tongs and belabours the fire.*] |
| Mena: | In the name of all that's dead and gone, wouldn't you take out your pipe and smoke it, not be humpin' yourself there, like a cat stealin' milk? |

[MENA *bends to take one of the buckets from under the working-table. She puts it between her boots and pours water from the full enamel drinking bucket into it. She replaces the enamel drinking bucket.*]

| Nanna: | [*Irritably:*] Such clatter! |

[MENA, *scoops several fistfuls of meal from the bag into the bucket.*]

| Mena: | No clatter unless 'tis your own. Wouldn't you give over talkin', and take out your pipe [*wearily*] and not be hiding it when we walk in and out of the kitchen? |
| Nanna: | Am I to be scolded, night and day in my own house? Ah! 'twas a sore day to me my son took you for a wife. What a happy home we had before you came into it! Fitter for you be having three of four children put from you at this day of your life. |
| Mena: | I had my fortune; 'twasn't for the want of a roof over my head that I came here. I could have done better if I bided my time. [*Lifts the bucket and turns to the door.*] |
| Nanna: | We all know what you could do, girl, and the stock you came from ... and the cabin you came out of! [*Laughs a little forcefully.*] Where ye used to drink yeer tay out of jam pots for the want of cups. Oh, indeed, you needn't tell me about yourself. A nice bargain you were! |
| Mena: | You have nothing else to do but talk. Saying your prayers you should be, at this hour of your days, |

instead of cackling with your bad tongue … Where was your poor amadawn of a son before I came here? Pulling bogdeal out of the ground with a jinnet, going around like a half-fool with his head hanging by him … you give me the puke with your grandeur. Take out your dirty doodeen of a pipe and close your gob on it, woman. I have something else to do besides arguing with you.

[MENA *lifts the latch to go out. As she does so, the door opens and a pretty young girl enters. She is aged about 18 and wears a grey tweed coat, a little too small for her. A flimsy scarf covers her head. She carries a satchel, filled with books, in her hand. Her name is* SIVE. *When she enters,* MENA *closes the door and looks at* SIVE *piercingly.* SIVE *puts her satchel on the large table, aware of* MENA'S *eyes upon her back.*]

**Sive:** I was held up after leaving the village. The front wheel of the bicycle went flat on me, and to crown my misfortune didn't I get a slow puncture in the other wheel. 'Tis the tyres that are worn. I was lucky to meet the master on the road. He gave me a lift as far as the end of the bohareen. [*She unties her scarf.*]

**Mena:** Schoolmasters and motor cars. And I suppose you expect me to have a hot dinner ready for you any minute of the day you decide to come home.

**Sive:** Oh, no! … we had a cookery class at the convent today, all the girls got dinner there. We had fricassee with dortois for dessert. It was lovely!

**Mena:** Saints preserve us! Out working with a farmer you should be, my girl, instead of getting your head filled with high notions. You'll come to no good either, like the one the went before you!

[MENA *lifts the bucket and goes out.* SIVE *takes off her coat and holds it over her arm. Underneath she wears a brown schoolgirl uniform with white collar attached.*]

**Sive:** What does she mean, Gran? The one that went before. Who was she referring to?

| | |
|---|---|
| **Nanna:** | There's no meaning to that woman's blather! [*Lifts her skirt and puts her pipe into her mouth.*] Quenched! bad skewer to her gone out! |
| **Sive:** | She meant my mother, didn't she, Gran? |
| **Nanna:** | [*Takes a box of matches from her pocket and lights her pipe.*] 'Sha your mother. |
| **Sive:** | Well, Gran, it was my mother, wasn't it? What did she mean? |
| **Nanna:** | Your mother, the Lord mercy on her, was my daughter. She wouldn't dare to draw down her name … it was only poison prattle, child; wind and steam. Isn't she always at it. 'Tis the disease in her system. If she didn't let it out of her mouth, 'twould break out in boils and sores all over her. You're worse, to take notice of her! |
| **Sive:** | [*Lays her coat over the books on the table and sits on its edge facing grandmother.*] Gran, all I know about my mother is that she died when I was a baby. Any time I've asked questions about her you've all put me off and told me you didn't know or that you had forgotten … and my father … you say he was drowned, no more. What I want to know is what sort of a man was he. Was he funny; was he handsome? Why wasn't he here by my mother's side when I was born or what kind of a father was he that he left her to suffer alone? |
| **Nanna:** | He was in England. He couldn't be here, could he, when he was there. He was drowned, the poor boy, a few days after you were born. Coal-mining he was, when the waters rushed in and trapped him. [*Reflective sadness.*] Away over in England. |
| **Sive:** | What was I like when I was born? Am I like my father now or like my mother? |
| **Nanna:** | Questions! Questions! Nothing but questions! You were a fine common lump of a baby! I remember well |

12

the night you were born. The doctor came in his new
motor car from the village. I remember well to see the
two roundy balls of fire coming up the bohareen. The
old people swore it was the devil but sure it was only
the two headlamps of the car shining in the darkness.
[*Draws on her pipe fruitlessly.*] Devil take the tobacco
they're making these days!

**Sive:** Tell me more about my mother, Gran. She was pretty,
wasn't she?

**Nanna:** [*With regret:*] She was pretty, too pretty. [*Shakes her
head.*] She was handsome, God rest her.

[*The kitchen door opens noiselessly and* Mena *stands framed in it without
speaking. She is unnoticed by* Sive *and* Nanna. *She carries the empty
bucket.*]

**Sive:** Go on, Gran! Tell me more! You must have so many
stories about my mother when she was young.

**Nanna:** What more is there to tell?

[*She lifts her head, looks past* Sive *to the door and tries to indicate to* Sive
*that* Mena *is at the door. She hides her pipe hurriedly. Suddenly* Sive
*understands and looks behind her in bewilderment. She comes to her feet
quickly.*]

**Mena:** 'Tis a wonder you took your backside from the table
where people do be eating. Is that what you're learning
at the convent?

[*Abashed,* Sive *takes her coat and books from the table.* Mena *puts the
bucket under the working-table.*]

**Mena:** Your uncle and I work ourselves to the marrow of the
bones to give you schooling and the minute I turn my
back you're cohackling with that oul' boody woman in
the corner. [*To* Nanna:] Some day that pipe will take
fire where you have it hidden and you'll go off in a big
black ball of smoke and ashes.

**Nanna:** [*Slowly:*] If I do, 'tis my prayer that the wind will blow
me in your direction and I'll have the satisfaction of

|  |  |
|---|---|
|  | taking you with me. Aha, you'd burn well, for you're as dry as the hobs of hell inside of you. Every woman of your age in the parish has a child of her own and nothing to show by you. |
| **Mena:** | Hold your tongue, old woman. How dare you cast your curses inside in my own house. It isn't my fault I have no child. [*Looks meaningly at* Sive.] Enough that had children in their time. I have every right to this house. I paid dear for my share. |
| **Nanna:** | I was here before you. |
| **Mena:** | Ah, but you won't be here after me! |
| **Nanna:** | That is the will of God, woman; not your will. |
| **Mena:** | [*To* Sive – *loudly:*] Take your books and get to your room. Is it for ornament you think we are keeping you? I'm sure the nuns would like to hear of your conduct. |

[Sive *hurries to the door at the right of kitchen. She casts a quick look behind her towards her grandmother.*]

|  |  |
|---|---|
| **Mena:** | What nonsense have you been filling the girl's head with? She'll be as cracked as the crows if she listens to you; wasting her time when she should be at her studies. When I was her age in my father's house I worked from dawn till dark to put aside my fortune. |
| **Nanna:** | You should have stayed in your father's house … Your father [*derisively*] a half starved bocock of a beggar with the Spanish blood galloping through his veins like litters of hungry greyhounds. |
| **Mena:** | [*Threateningly:*] Old woman, be careful with your free tongue! 'Twill wither up inside your head. You mind your corner of the house and I'll mind mine. You have great gumption for a woman with nothing. |
| **Nanna:** | [*Takes the tongs in her hand.*] The calves are bawling for their milk. |

14

[NANNA *leans on the tongs and rises with its support, then lets it fall noisily. She goes after* SIVE *into the room at the right of kitchen, ignoring* MENA's *looks. She walks slightly humped.*

*When she has left,* MENA *goes to the fire and rearranges it with the tongs. She goes to the dresser, opens one of the doors and extracts an apron which she ties about her waist. Going to fire she lifts the skillet from the crane and replaces it with the kettle. She uses the hem of her apron to handle both utensils. She goes to the working-table and withdraws the second bucket, and listens at door of room where* NANNA *and* SIVE *are.*

*While she is thus occupied there is a faint knock on the kitchen door. She turns instantly, then looks into the mirror and pats her hair hurriedly. She advances a step towards the door.*]

**Mena:** Come in, let you!

[*The door opens slowly and a man peers cautiously about the kitchen. He wears a disfigured felt hat upon unruly hair and looks as if he had not shaved for a week. He is shifty-looking, ever on his guard. He is fortyish. He takes the hat from his head and thrusts it into his coat pocket, when his eyes rest on* MENA. *He is* THOMASHEEN SEÁN RUA, *a matchmaker.*]

**Thomasheen:** Are you along, bean a' tighe? [*He looks around again.*] Or is there someone with you? [*Very confidential. His voice has a rasp-like quality with the calculated slow drawl typical of the south-west.*]

**Mena:** I'm as much alone as ever I'll be. Come in, will you. You look like a scarecrow there in the doorway.

**Thomasheen:** God help us, amn't I like a scarecrow always, match-making and making love between people I spend my days and no thanks for it.

[*He enters and goes to the fire. He turns his back to it and lifts the tail of his overcoat to savour the heat.* MENA *closes the door and stands at the table.*]

**Mena:** [*Pause.*] What is all the secrecy about, Thomasheen. You look like you have something to tell.

**Thomasheen:** There's a frightful sting in the air this evening. There is the sign of rain to the west, God between us and all harm … Is the man of the house within or without?

15

**Mena:** He is gone to the village with a rail of bonhams.

**Thomasheen:** Ah! Great money in bonhams these days. They'll save the country yet, I may tell you. There's more money in two bonhams than there is in the making of a match, God help us.

**Mena:** If you think I can spend the evening listening to bualam ski, you can go the road for yourself. What is that brought you? Out with it!

**Thomasheen:** There is no one with an ear cocked? [*He looks about suspiciously.*]

**Mena:** The old woman and the girl are below in the room but you can shout to the heavens for all the attention they'll pay to you. If it is after matchmaking you came, boy, you have put pains on your feet for nothing.

**Thomasheen:** Thomasheen Seán Rua never blisters his feet without cause. There is some one who have a great wish for the young lady, this one they call Sive. 'Tis how he have seen her bicycling to the convent in the village. [*Shakes his head solemnly.*] He is greatly taken by her. He have the mouth half-open when he do be talking about her. 'Tis the sign of love, women!

**Mena:** Are you by any chance taking leave of your senses, buachall! What is she but a schoolgirl … and illegitimate, to crown all! She has no knowledge of her father and the mother is dead with shame out of her the most of twenty years.

**Thomasheen:** Illegitimate! There is fierce bond to the word and great length to it. Whatever she is, she has the makings of a woman.

**Mena:** Rameish! You have great talk.

**Thomasheen:** Ah! but she have one thing we will never see any more of, God help us … she have the youth and the figure and the face to stand over it. 'Tis the youth, blast you, that the old men do be after. 'Tis the heat [*pronounced 'hait'*] before death that plays upon them.

**Mena:** Old men! What are you saying about old men! [*Her voice rises in volume.*]

**Thomasheen:** Hush, woman! … You'll tell the parish! … What matter if the girl be what she is, if she had a black face and the hooves of a pony … the man I mention is taken with her. He will buy, sell and lose all to have her. He have the wish for the girl.

**Mena:** [*Suddenly shrewd:*] Who has the wish for her?

**Thomasheen:** No quibble between the pair of us, Mena. Seán Dóta is the man.

**Mena:** Seán Dóta!

**Thomasheen:** Hould your hoult, woman! Take heed of what I say. He have the grass of twenty cows. He have fat cattle besides and he have the holding of money.

**Mena:** He's as old as the hills!

**Thomasheen:** But he's a hardy thief with the mad mind for women breaking out through him like the tetter with no cure for it. What matter if he is as grey as the goat. There is many a young man after a year of marriage losing his heart for love-making. This man have the temper. He would swim the Shannon for a young wife. He would spoil her, I tell you. There is good reward for all concerned in it. Don't be hasty, to be sorry later.

**Mena:** You are like all the matchmakers: you will make a rose out of a nettle to make a bargain.

**Thomasheen:** He have the house to himself – nothing to be done by her only walk in and take charge. There is a servant boy and a servant girl. There is spring water in the back yard, and a pony and trap for going to the village.

**Mena:** Seán Dóta! [*Reflectively:*] The girl hasn't a brown penny to her name.

| Thomasheen: | No fortune is wanted, I tell you. 'Tis how he will give money to have her. |
|---|---|
| Mena: | He will give money! The devil isn't your master for the red lies. That's the first I ever heard of a farmer giving money instead of looking for it. What will we hear next? |
| Thomasheen: | [*Extends both hands.*] 'Tis the ageing blood in the thief … Ah! It's an old story, girl. The old man and the young woman. When they get the stroke this way there is no holding them. There is the longing he have been storing away these years past. |
| Mena: | [*Pause.*] And you say he would give money for her? |
| Thomasheen: | That my right hand might fall off if he won't! Two hundred sovereigns for you if the girl will consent. |
| Mena: | [*Suspiciously:*] And what is for you? It isn't out of the goodness of yer heart you are playing your hand. |
| Thomasheen: | There will be £100 for me. |
| Mena: | £200 … she'll scorn him. She has high notions. |
| Thomasheen: | Aye! It won't come aisy. [*He advances a little way towards her and lowers his head to peer at her before going on.*] High notions, or no high notions, you're the one that can do it. Isn't she a bye-child? … Tell her you will bell-rag her through the parish if she goes against you. Tell her you will hunt the oul' woman into the county home. Think of the 200 sovereigns dancing in the heel of your fist. Think of the thick bundle of notes in the shelter of your bosom. It isn't every day of the week £200 will come your way. |
| Mena: | The girl is flighty like a colt. Threats might only make her worse. |
| Thomasheen: | Be silky then, be canny! Take her gentle. Let it out to her by degrees. Draw down the man's name first by way of no harm. You could mention the fine place he have. You could say he would be for the grave within |

a year or two and that she might pick and choose from the bucks of the parish when he's gone.

**Mena:** She'll cock her nose at him! ... 'Tis all love and romancing these days with little thought for comfort or security. [*Pause.*] Twenty cows and money to burn! [*Reflectively:*] She'll do no better for all her airs and graces. Look at the match I made ... four cows on the side of a mountain and a few acres of bog.

**Thomasheen:** Remember there's 200 sovereigns staring you in the face if you will be doing your duty by Seán Dóta.

**Mena:** I will consider [*Pause.*] ... The old woman would be against it. She has the charming of the girl in her hands. They are as thick as thieves, the pair of them.

**Thomasheen:** Gently will do it, step by step. Show her the chances she will have, the fine clothes and the envy of the neighbours. The house is like a bishop's palace, paper on every wall, and a pot, by all accounts, under every bed. She will have the life of a queen.

**Mena:** [*Thoughtfully:*] And I would be rid of her. And £200 into the bargain. I would!

**Thomasheen:** And you would be rid of the old woman, too.

**Mena:** [*Alert:*] By what way?

**Thomasheen:** We will make it a part of the match that she will go with Sive.

**Mena:** I would be clear and clane of the pair of 'em!

**Thomasheen:** 'Tis a chance that will not pass the way again.

**Mena:** Would he take the oul' woman, do you think?

**Thomasheen:** Do you know the man you have? How many years is Seán Dóta in the world? How many years have he spent searchin' the country for a young woman?

**Mena:** Will he take the oul' woman or won't he?

**Thomasheen:** He will have anything, I tell you, if he will get Sive.

| | |
|---|---|
| **Mena:** | It would be a great day to the house. Years I have suffered with the two of them, always full of hate for me. I would give my right hand to have that oul' hag out of my way. |
| **Thomasheen:** | Ah, you have no life, God help us, with the worry of them. |
| **Mena:** | Why should that young rip be sent to a convent every day instead of being out earning with a farmer. Good money going on her because her fool of a mother begged on the death-bed to educate her. |
| **Thomasheen:** | 'Tis a mortal sin! |
| **Mena:** | 'Tis worse! 'Tis against nature. She'll have her eyes opened. |
| **Thomasheen:** | I often wonder how you put up with it at all. |
| **Mena:** | I won't suffer long more. |
| **Thomasheen:** | [*Rubs his hands gleefully.*] I knew my woman from the start. You must go to the core of the apple to come by the seed. |
| **Mena:** | Himself? … What will he say? |
| **Thomasheen:** | Aren't ye in the one bed sleeping? Ye will have yeer own talk. You will come around him aisy. You weren't born a fool, Mena. I know what it is like in the long long hours of the night. I know what it is to be alone in a house when the only word you will hear is a sigh, the sigh of the fire in the hearth dying, with no human words to warm you. I am a single man. [*Deadly serious:*] I know what a man have to do who have no woman to lie with him. He have to drink hard, or he have to walk under the black sky when every eye is closed in sleep. Now, with you, there is a difference. You have the man. You have the companion. Sleeping or waking you have your husband in the flesh and bone and there is the one will between ye. You will see |

that he is of the same word as yourself. Be said by me, leanav [*ingratiatingly*], take the rough with the smooth ... But have your way. Keep the picture of 200 sovereigns in your mind.

**Mena:** [*Calculatingly:*] Aisy said!

**Thomasheen:** [*Touches her hand.*] There is the money to think of. [*He withdraws his hand immediately, and going to window, looks out.*] No sign of rail and car. [*He looks at* MENA.] Listen, woman, I will call tonight with my man, just as if we were passing the way by chance. Pretend nothing!

[*Suddenly the room door at stage right opens noisily and* NANNA *comes in.*]

**Mena:** What is all the fuastar for? Is it how the hinges of the door are worn? Or must you make noise wherever you go with the bitterness that's in you?

[NANNA *does not answer but goes to the dresser and takes a cup. Slowly, deliberately, she goes to where the milk-tank is. Looking over at* THOMASHEEN *she lifts its cover and dips a cup inside it. She withdraws the cup, having filled it, and replaces the cover.*]

**Mena:** The top of the tank for her ladyship!

**Nanna:** Would you see the girl hungry? [*To* THOMASHEEN:] I know you, Thomasheen Seán Rua. 'Tis no good that brings you here this day of the week. The mean snap is in you and all that went before you. You'd sell your soul to the devil for a drink of buttermilk.

[THOMASHEEN *advances, fists clenched, but holds his tongue. He glares at the old woman, who turns and goes into the room again.*]

**Thomasheen:** Ah-ha! hag! consumptive oul' hag! Seed an' breed of consumptive oul' hags. [*His voice grows high-pitched. To* MENA:] Marry the young one and be rid of that oul' devil!

**Mena:** Huist! ... I hear the axle of a car on the road ... 'tis himself coming from the village. [*Becomes flurried.*]

Clear away with you … tonight, mind! I will come around himself in my own time. He has a great love for the few pounds.

**Thomasheen:** [*Goes to door, and peeps out. Then turns to* MENA.] I'll have the old man here by nightfall.

[THOMASHEEN *opens the door, looks to left and right and disappears.* MENA *takes three plates and cups from dresser and puts them on table. Goes to the tankard of milk and fills a jug by immersing it. She dries the jug with her apron and fills the three cups with milk. From lower part of dresser she takes three large spoons, and puts them on the table. Between each action she looks out of window. When the door opens,* MENA *does not turn to look at the new arrival. He is her husband,* MIKE GLAVIN. *Under his arm he carries a sack partly filled with hay which he puts under the working-table. He carries a thonged whip attached to an ash-plant. He is a quiet man, determined of movement. His voice will be studious and calculated.*]

**Mena:** You're back!

**Mike:** Aye!

[*He goes immediately to table and sits on the chair nearest to it. The man of the house is home! The woman must become alert in her own way.* MIKE *searches his right-hand pocket. He withdraws a few currency notes and some silver. He places them on the nearest of the three plates. He smooths the notes awkwardly with his fingers, folds them, and begins to count the silver with inexperienced hands. With a single gesture he returns the money to his pocket.*]

**Mena:** How much today?

**Mike:** What have you in the skillet?

**Mena:** How much money did you make?

**Mike:** [*He does not move his head.*] £16 10s. I gave a crown luck.

**Mena:** How much for the single bonham?

**Mike:** 'Twas together I sold them.

**Mena:** A great day's hire! Will it last?

**Mike:** 'Twill last! [*Pause.*] It makes a great change from beggin' and pinchin' with our craws often only half-filled. Ah! you should see the shopkeepers in the village today. Like singing birds they were, calling out our names when we passed with our loads. [*Noisily:*] I mind a day not so long past when they had us by the throats. They wouldn't give a half-sack of flour without money down. The boot is on the other foot now with turf the way it is and pigs and calves fetching the high price. It does the heart good to see the shopkeepers scrapin' and bowin'. Money is the best friend a man ever had. [*He takes off his coat and hands it from a crook behind kitchen door.*]

**Mena:** We will mind whatever penny we make.

**Mike:** You may say we'll mind it! [*He puts his hand into pocket of coat and withdraws the money, which he hands to* MENA.] What have you to ate, woman?

[MENA *does not answer his question immediately but wraps the notes about the silver coins and transfers the lot to the pocket of her skirt.*]

**Mena:** The spuds are boiled. I will make a muller of onion dip. Sit down a tamaill. There is something I have to say to you.

**Mike:** [*Puzzled:*] Yes … what?

**Mena:** Sit here! [*She indicates the chair which he has vacated. He sits on it looking at her expectantly.*] It is about Sive.

**Mike:** Sive!

[MENA *sits at the left of the table and places her hands on it.*]

**Mike:** What is it about Sive?

**Mena:** How will I start to tell you? [*Pauses.*] There is an account of a match for Sive.

**Mike:** [*Screws up his face in wonder.*] For Sive? … a match? Are you going simple, woman? There is no sense or meaning to you. She's only a child … still going to school …

23

**Mena:** [*Crossly:*] She's old enough! The grass of twenty cows, a farm free of debt; money rotting there.

**Mike:** She has no fortune. What farmer of that size would take her without money?

**Mena:** He'll be glad to have her, money or no. Think of twenty milch cows and security for the rest of her days.

**Mike:** She is different. She has book-learning. She will turn a deaf ear to matchmaking. [*He shakes his head.*] I'm her uncle. When my sister died I gave my word that I would stand by her. The girl is too young. She has no father. I have responsibility.

**Mena:** Was it your fault, I ask you, that your sister died? Was it your fault that she gave birth to the girl or was too free with men? [*In anger.*]

**Mike:** [*Warning:*] Aisy, a-girl! [*Deadly note:*] Aisy! She was young in the ways of the world. She paid dearly for her folly, God help us. She dressed a thorny bed for herself. Will you look how old the world is and how the youth do be so foolish in it.

**Mena:** Now listen to me! [*Insistent:*] The child was born in want of wedlock. That much is well known from one end of the parish to the other. What is before her when she can put no name on her father? What better can she do when the chance of comfort is calling to her. Will you take stock of yourself, man! There is a fine farm waiting her with servants to tend her so that her hands will be soft and clean when the women of the parish will be up to their eyes in cow dung and puddle. What better can she do? Who will take her with the slur and the doubt hanging over her?

**Mike:** [*Shakes his head.*] I don't know, woman! I don't know what is best.

**Mena:** You know as well as I do that what I say is best for the girl.

**Mike:**     Maybe so! … Maybe so! [*Puzzled:*] But who is the man who would marry without a fortune and he having that fine bane of cows?

[MENA *is silent for a moment, looking at him from beneath lowered brows.*]

**Mike:**     Well?

**Mena:**     [*Pauses, then looks directly at him.*] Seán Dóta from the foot of the hill.

**Mike:**     [*Open-mouthed, repeating the words slowly.*] Seán Dóta!

**Mena:**     [*Hurriedly:*] A respectable man with a good bit put away by him. And it will mean that we will be rid of your mother, too. Sive will take her for company. Wouldn't it be wonderful?

[MIKE *suddenly jumps to his feet.*]

**Mike:**     Never! … if the sun, moon and stars rained down out of the heavens and split the ground under my feet … never! 'Twill never come to pass while I have the pulse of life in me! [*Changes his tone from anger to entreaty.*] What devil has got into you that you should think of such a thing? Even when I was a boy Seán Dóta was a man. The grave he should be thinking of. What young girl would look a second time at him, a worn, exhausted little lurgadawn of a man.

**Mena:**     You are hasty to condemn! Will you sit down and hear me out. We will have the house here to ourselves with the oul' woman gone as well. [*Suggested note of love.*]

**Mike:**     [*Loud voiced:*] Never! Not even if the Son of God walked the roads of the earth again! She will not darken the door of his house.

**Mena:**     Will you sit down, man. You will take flight! Sit here!

**Mike:**     Sit for what …? Sit, is it, to give ear to the greatest nonsense within the four walls of the world! You can't be in your right mind.

25

**Mena:** There is the gift of £200 for us if there is a marriage. [*Long pause.*] Think of the start it would give us. How many times would you bend your back to make it? Long enough we were scraping: you said it yourself. Consider it, will you? It is what we wanted always. Sive will be well off and we will be rid of your mother and her taunting.

**Mike:** No! No! A million thousand times no! It would sleep with me for the rest of my days. It would be like tossing the white flower of the canavaun on to the manure heap. It is against the grain of my bones, woman. Will you think of it? Think of what it is! Sive and that oul' corpse of a man, Seán Dóta!

**Mena:** [*Soothing motherly tone:*] Will you sit down and be said by me.

**Mike:** I will not sit! … I am going out!

**Mena:** [*Repeating his words, her voice filled with sarcasm:*] You are going out! [*Changes to a tone of boldness:*] Well, if you are going out, I am going with you.

**Mike:** [*Lifts his right hand.*] There is a finish, girl, to our talk. Leave me to myself. I have a wish to go by myself. Let me be. [*He looks at her, filled with doubt.*]

**Mena:** [*Pause.*] Go away! Go away with you. Go away, man of straw.

**Mike:** [*Harshly, loud-voiced:*] I am no man of straw. Will you not leave me be with myself?

[*Suddenly, in a violent fit of temper, he knocks over the chair upon which he has been sitting and goes out, slamming the door. MENA rises and follows him through the door, leaving it open after her, still calling his name.*

*When both are gone, the old woman comes from the room and looks out after them. She goes to the fire, produces her pipe and lights it. She has only just sat down when a young man enters; aged about nineteen, he is good-looking and manly, his voice cultured and refined. His entrance is somewhat hurried. He is LIAM SCUAB. He carries a few short planks and a bag of tools.*]

| | |
|---|---|
| **Liam:** | I never saw such commotion. First I saw Thomasheen Seán Rua, the matchmaker, sneaking away over the mountain from this house. Next I saw Mike hurrying out of here as if the devil were after him and, last of all I saw Mena running after Mike, calling his name. What's going on at all? Have they all gone mad? [*He puts his tools and planks on table.*] |
| **Nanna:** | You'd better not be caught here. There will be trouble. Mike Glavin has no liking for you or any of yours, Liam. |
| **Liam:** | I wouldn't have called only I was sure there was nobody here but Sive and yourself. I was up the road making a door for Seamus Dónal. Where is she? |
| **Nanna:** | [*Archly:*] Where is who? |
| **Liam:** | [*Smiling:*] Come on, you oul' schemer! You know who I mean. |
| **Nanna:** | [*Rises and calls to* Sive's *room.*] Sive, Liam Scuab is here. |

[Sive *enters.*]

| | |
|---|---|
| **Sive:** | Liam! … what brought you? |
| **Liam:** | I was passin' by; just going the road on business. |
| **Sive:** | [*Suddenly alarmed, breaks away.*] You'll be caught! [*To* Nanna:] Where is Mena … my Uncle Mike … He'll have a fit, Liam! |
| **Nanna:** | Be careful, let ye, and keep a watch. If 'tis a thing ye're caught together there'll be no more peace in his house. [*Exit* Nanna.] |
| **Liam:** | [*Taking* Sive's *hand.*] Will you be able to steal out tonight? |
| **Sive:** | If I can, but if I don't come at the time, don't wait. |
| **Liam:** | I'll wait till the crack of dawn, anyway. |
| **Sive:** | Be careful. Uncle Mike hates you. |
| **Liam:** | What harm if he does. He might as well hate me as anybody. |

| | |
|---|---|
| **Sive:** | [*Pause.*] I wonder what Mena and Uncle Mike are doing in the bog? |
| **Liam:** | Who knows? I saw Thomasheen Seán Rua, the matchmaker, leaving here too, a while back. |
| **Sive:** | Thomasheen Seán Rua! What did that devil want? |
| **Liam:** | Nothing good, I'll warrant. Imagine making a marriage between two people who never saw each other before. |
| **Sive:** | Horrible? |
| **Liam:** | They say it is necessary in country places. |
| **Sive:** | It's horrible, Liam. Would you marry somebody you never saw before? |
| **Liam:** | I would marry nobody but you, Sive, I love you. How would I marry anybody but you! |
| **Sive:** | [*Pause.*] You'd better go. If we're found together …! |
| **Liam:** | [*Takes his possessions from table.*] I'll wait tonight until you come. |
| **Sive:** | If I don't come when I say, go home. It's cold and lonely waiting in the dark. |
| **Liam:** | It's cold and lonely, too, at home. |
| **Sive:** | Look, if I don't come, I'll meet you on the road from school tomorrow. |
| **Liam:** | Try to come if you can. |

[MIKE *enters angrily.*]

| | |
|---|---|
| **Mike:** | What's this? [*Louder:*] What's this, I say. What are you doing in my house, Liam Scuab? How dare one of your breed cross my door in! |
| **Sive:** | [*Timorously:*] He was passing by! |
| **Mike:** | He was passing by! He was! He was, like a rat when he saw the nest empty. He came stealing and sneaking when we were outside. |

| | |
|---|---|
| **Sive:** | He was not sneaking and he was not stealing. |
| **Mike:** | Go to your room … Go on! [*Exit* SIVE.] |
| **Liam:** | [*Calmly:*] No blame to Sive. |
| **Mike:** | I know your breed, Scuab, and what you are and I know what you're looking for. |
| **Liam:** | There's no need to sound so dirty about it. |
| **Mike:** | I know what you're after, Scuab. |
| **Liam:** | [*Calmly:*] I make no denial about it. I'm after Sive. |
| **Mike:** | I know well what you're after. |
| **Liam:** | You know one thing and I know another. I say I am after Sive and nothing more than that. I love her. |
| **Mike:** | Like your snake of a cousin loved her mother moryeah and fooled her likewise. Like your snake of a cousin that tricked her mother with the promise of marriage and left her a child with no name. |
| **Liam:** | [*Calmly:*] I know who Sive's father is. It is no fault of mine. |
| **Mike:** | It was the fault of your cousin and ye're the one breed. |
| **Liam:** | You know as well as I do that he would have married her. You know he went across to England to make a home for her but he was drowned. He never knew she was with child when he left. |
| **Mike:** | You bring your tale well, don't you? Quick words and book-readin' like all belonging to you. Like your bloody cousin. |
| **Liam:** | He died, didn't he? What more do you want? |
| **Mike:** | I want for you to leave here and keep away from Sive. I want that you should never set eyes on her again or you will pay as dear as your cousin paid, maybe. |
| **Liam:** | You will not command the lives and happiness of two people who love each other. |

**Mike:**        *[In a rage:]* I will not command … the cheek … go on, get out of here, you upstart … Go on! … Go!

**Liam:**        *[Pause – exiting.]* We shall see.

**Mike:**        *[Roaring:]* Go on, you tathaire, go on …

*[Exit* LIAM *waving a hand behind his back in disgust. When he has gone* MIKE *fumes in the kitchen. After a moment he goes to the door and calls* MENA.*]*

**Mike:**        Mena! … Mena! …

*[*MIKE *exits calling her name.]*

## CURTAIN

# SCENE 2

[*The time: night. A paraffin lamp burns on a shelf over the fireplace.*
SIVE, MIKE *and* MENA *are in the kitchen.*

MIKE *is seated by the fire. In his lap is a pony's collar much worn and patched. With a heavy bent shoemaker's needle he stitches a piece of sacking on it.*

SIVE *is seated at the table at end furthest from* MIKE. *Her satchel of books stands open on the table. Her head is bent over a book from which she is memorising* sotto voce.

MENA *stands over the working-table, her sleeves rolled up, her back turned to the other two. She is washing a shirt in a tin basin. She takes the shirt from basin, squeezes it dry and places it on the table. She takes the basin in her hand, goes to door, opens it and throws the dirty water out; closing the door she turns to* MIKE.]

**Mena:**     The dogs are barking at the end of the bohareen. Someone is coming the road.

[MIKE *does not look up from his work.* SIVE *looks abstractedly towards* MENA *and then to her book again.* MENA *places the basin on the working-table and pours some water into it from the drinking pail. She takes the shirt and begins to rinse it again in the basin. She turns as though to say something, but changes her mind and continues with her washing.* SIVE *closes the book, puts it in the bag, takes another. She opens it and continues to memorise part of it. There is a knock at the door.* MENA *goes to the door and asks.*]

**Mena:**     Who is out?

**Voice:**     [*Off, sonorous, high-pitched:*] Thomasheen Seán Rua and Seán Dóta from the butt of the hill. Doing a bit of rambling we are.

**Mena:**     Come in, let you!

[*The door opens and* THOMASHEEN *looks around the kitchen shiftily. He exchanges the barest of glances with* SIVE *who looks at him curiously. He looks cautiously at* MIKE *who ignores him, then at* MENA *who nods to him.* THOMASHEEN *turns and with a motion of his head calls* SEÁN DÓTA. *He enters the kitchen followed by* SEÁN. THOMASHEEN *makes straight for the fire and turns his back to it, lifting his coat-tails to warm himself.*]

**Thomasheen**: [*Shudders.*] God save all here. Brr! There is a cold there tonight that would peel the skin from your back. [*To* SEÁN DÓTA, *in a mild pleasing tone:*] Come away in from the cold, Seán achree. There is a black wind coming around the shoulder of the mountain with fangs in it like the tooth of a boar.

[SEÁN DÓTA *advances, shyly, a little ways. He looks for a moment gloatingly at* SIVE, *and smiling shyly looks to* THOMASHEEN.

SEÁN *is a small man, a little wizened. His age might be anything from 55 to 70. He takes off a bright-coloured cap and holds it supplicatingly in front of him. His hair is whitish-grey worn in a fringe at his forehead. His eyes are birdlike, shrewd. He wears a respectable frieze overcoat which seems too large for him.*]

**Mena:** You're welcome here, Seán Dóta. Will you sit up to the fire and let the heat draw the cold out of your bones?

**Seán Dóta:** No, thanks, Mrs Glavin. I will sit here by the dresser. I'd not like to come in the way of anyone.

[*His voice is apologetic. Whenever he speaks he also smiles with a half laugh as if to excuse himself. He sits on a chair by the dresser. He leans forward expectantly with his palms on his knees.*]

**Thomasheen:** The heat don't agree with him. He would sooner a cold corner out of the way. [SEÁN DÓTA *nods with a half laugh in agreement with* THOMASHEEN.] He have a very aisy-going manner with him. He have the health of a spring salmon, that man have. You wouldn't like to meet him, he's so nice. [SEÁN DÓTA *nods modestly.*]

[MIKE *holds the collar out at arm's length to examine it.* THOMASHEEN *watches interestedly.*]

**Thomasheen:** You're a great hand for mendin'! There's a drop of the cobbler's blood in your veins, Mike, boy! 'Tis a

32

joy to watch you with the needle. [MIKE *gives him a withering look.*]

**Mike:** [*To* MENA:] Maybe they might have mind for a mouthful of tay?

**Mena:** The kettle is very near the boil.

[SIVE *begins to gather her books. Both of the new arrivals protest vigorously at the idea of tea.*]

**Seán:** We're only just after rising from the table. 'Twould be a waste. We're thankful, all the same.

**Mena:** 'Tis there in plenty if ye have a mind for it.

**Thomasheen:** Too good you are, woman, to put yourself out for us. [*He goes to the table and stands over* SIVE. *He looks at the book in front of her. Then to the house at large he says:*] Ah, the book-learning is a wonderful thing. Many is the time I have regrets for the idleness of my youth. What a nate curate I would make, or a canon, maybe, in time with the shoes shining by me night and morning. 'Tis a wise man that puts himself out for the learning. [*To* SIVE, *cajolingly:*] And what is it you have in the book there before you?

**Sive:** Poetry and verses.

**Thomasheen:** Ah! [*Exhilaratingly:*] Poetry ... God help us, 'tis far from the poetry book I was reared. There is a verse out of the end of a poem now, I heard a tinker woman reciting back the years. The way it goes ...

[*He cocks his head and purses his lips, then in a stentorian voice almost bawdy in tone, he begins:*]

> The ripest apple is the soonest rotten;
> The hottest love is the soonest cold ...

[*Out of the corner of his eye he surveys* SIVE.]

> ... and a young man's vows, they are soon forgotten;
> Go away, young man, do not make so bold!
> Ah, poetry is a gift from the angels of Heaven!

33

[MENA *squeezes the shirt, puts it aside, opens the door, and empties the basin.*]

**Mike:** [*Politely:*] Have you a liking for the versifying, Seán?

[MENA *replaces the basin and folds her hands. She stands approvingly at the end of the kitchen behind* SIVE.]

**Seán Dóta:** Divil the bit, Mike. I have nothing against the poets, mind you, but they are filled with roguery and they have the bad tongue on top of it, the thieves. Oh, the scoundrels!

**Mena:** Have you e'er a poem, Seán? You must have great verses by you, a man with your gentlemanly nature.

**Seán Dóta:** Oho! [*Deprecatingly, laughs and shakes his head.*]

**Thomasheen:** Ah, he's as deep as a well, woman! As wise as a book! As sharp as a scythe! There's no telling the verses he have.

**Mena:** Give us a rann out of one of them. I'll bet anything 'tis the best that was ever heard.

[SIVE *is amazed at* SEÁN's *voice and manner.* SEÁN *looks at her keenly.*]

**Seán Dóta:** Begor, then, I will say a verse for the girl. It was from my grandfather I brought it. [*Shifts on his seat.*] A very tasty handful of poetry too, it is.

[*He coughs, bringing his hand to his mouth delicately. In a sing-song voice, very high in tone, he starts:*]

> Seánín Easter, di-do-dom,
> Stole a pratey from his mom.
> He was caught and he was hung.
> He was buried in the dung.
> When the dung was piking out
> He was hopping like a trout.
> When the dung was piking in
> He was hopping like a hen.

[MENA *acclaims him loudly, as do* THOMASHEEN *and* MIKE. SEÁN *shakes his head bashfully, giving the half-laugh again.*]

**Mena:**  [*Feigning delight:*] Well, isn't he the devil's own!

**Thomasheen:**  Ah! he have the humour all over him.

**Mike:**  'Twas lively, faix!

[MIKE *rises, having completed his work on the collar. He places it against the dresser and goes to his seat again.*]

**Mena:**  Sive, child [*gently*], there's a small journey for you. [*Full of supplication, she comes to where* SIVE *is sitting. Her manner is pleading, yet considerate.*] There's a favour. [*Pause.*] Didn't the laths of the rail burst with the weight of turf. Would you by any chance go the road down to the butt of the bohareen to Seamus Dónal's cottage. Tell him we want the loan of a rail for the morning. He is working in the quarry and sure he'll have no need of it himself. You can tell him it will be called for with the dawn.

**Sive:**  [*Resignedly:*] I'll go!

**Mena:**  [*To the house in general:*] She's a gift for obliging. [*Her voice is all praise.*] She would turn on her heel from whatever she is at, to be of help. [*She helps* SIVE *on with her coat.*]

**Sive:**  [*Reflectively – looking up at* MENA *childishly:*] To be called for at the dawn. I am to tell him the rail was burst with the weight of turf.

**Mena:**  And thank him for the use of it.

[SIVE *goes to the dresser for her scarf.*]

**Thomasheen:**  Well, it's a strange thing that I will be going home by the short cut across the mountain. It was only to keep me company on the road that Seán came as far as this with me. It would be nice for the girl to have his company as far as the foot of the bohareen. [*Looking around with wide innocent eyes:*] And sure 'twould

|             |                                                                                                      |
|-------------|------------------------------------------------------------------------------------------------------|
|             | be company for him too. A young heart is a great companion on the road.                               |
| Sive:       | There is no need for Mr Dóta to come with me. I know the road well enough from walking it every day.  |

**Thomasheen:** Of course you do, who would know it better? [*Questions the company as if defying contradiction:*] But think of the dark, girl, and the phuca [*pauses*], the mad, red eyes of him like coals of fire lighting in his head. There is no telling what you would meet on a black road. There's a mad moon in the sky tonight with the stars out of their mind screeching and roaring at one another.

**Seán Dóta:** [*Rises from the chair.*] I'll be as far as Seamus Dónal's with her. There will no one cross her path with Seán Dóta walking by her side. [*Apologetic laugh.*]

**Sive:** [*Indignantly:*] I am not afraid of the dark, or the phuca!

**Thomasheen:** Ah, sure, you would be like a hare on the road with the tidy little white feet of you.

**Seán:** It's as well to be going … I have the notion of buying a motoring car [*to impress* Sive]. It is all the fashion these days … very saving on the feet. [*Again, the apologetic half-laugh.*] By all accounts the women do be driving them, too.

[Seán *leads the way out, followed by* Sive *who looks irritated at the thought of* Seán's *company.*]

**Seán:** Good night all, and God bless!

**Thomasheen:** Good night. God bless.

[Thomasheen *runs silently to the door, opens it noiselessly and peeps out after them.* Mena *advances to the fire and stands at one side of it watching* Thomasheen. Mike *and* Mena *exchange glances.* Thomasheen *closes door and turns, rubbing hands gleefully.*]

**Thomasheen:** The seed is sown; the flower will blossom.

**Mena:** [*Sits opposite* Mike *and faces* Thomasheen.] The old woman mustn't know … the girl will know in good time … No need to tell her. It will come over her like a summer tide.

[THOMASHEEN *sits facing the fire and runs his fingers through his wild hair, head bent.*]

**Mike:** I can't folly with ye! If there was less between them in the years it would be a great day's work. She'll never take with him. It's too much to ask of her.

**Mena:** Are you forgetting the money? There is a soft bone somewhere in your head, man. And are you forgetting this evening and Liam Scuab?

**Mike:** I know! I know! The money is a great temptation but there is wrong in it from head to heel. Sive is young, with a brain by her. She will be dreaming about love with a young man. 'Tis the way the young girls do be!

**Thomasheen:** [*Comes nearer* MIKE *and extends his hands.*] Will you listen to him! Love! In the name of God, what do the likes of us know about love? [*Turns to* MENA *and points a finger at* MIKE.] Did you ever hear the word of love on his lips? Ah, you did not, girl! [THOMASHEEN *rises to the occasion.*] Did he ever give you a little rub behind the ear or run his fingers through your hair and tell you that he would swim the Shannon for you? Did he ever sing the love-songs for you in the far-out part of the night when ye do be alone? [THOMASHEEN *scoffs.*] He would sooner to stick his snout in a plate of mate and cabbage, or to rub the back of a fattening pig than whisper a bit of his fondness for you. Do he run to you when he come in from the bog and put his arms around you and give you a big smohawnach of a kiss and tell you that the length of the day was like the length of a million years while he was separated from you? [*In triumph:*] Could you say that he ever brought you the token of a brooch or a bit of finery? … Naa! More likely a few pence worth

37

o' musty sweets if the drink made him foolish of a fair day. [*Scornfully:*] And to hear you blatherin' about love! The woman would think you were out of your mind if you put a hand around her on the public road. [MIKE *looks hang-dog.*]

**Mena:** You are no one to talk!

**Thomasheen:** I make no boast either. What I say is what business have the likes of us with love? It is enough to have to find the bite to eat. When I was a young man, 20 years ago, my father, God rest him, put a finish to my bit of love.

**Mena:** [*In unbelief:*] You had love?

**Thomasheen:** I had a wish for a girl from the other side of the mountain. But what was the good when I had no place to take her. There was a frightful curam of us in my father's house with nothing but a sciath of spuds on the floor to fill us. I had two pigs fattening. [*Lonesome:*] My father was an amadawn, a stump of a fool who took his life by his own hand. He hung himself from a tree near the house. I swear to you he would never have hanged himself but he knew my two pigs would pay for his wake and funeral. 'Twas the meanness in his heart, for he knew well I had my heart set on marriage.

**Mena:** What a lonesome story you have for us.

**Thomasheen:** Not so lonesome now! There's a widow-woman having a small place beyond the village. £100 would see me settled in with her.

**Mike:** She will be blessed by you! Will you give her the rub behind the ear? Will you give her brooches and clothes? Ha-ha! I would like to see it!

**Thomasheen:** Give over! ... [*To* MENA:] There is this young Scuab who have a heart for the girl. He will have fine words for her, looking like a gentleman, with his collar and tie and his poll plastered with hair-*oil* [*accent on 'oil'*].

|   |   |
|---|---|
|  | I have seen him, after his day's work, looking like a play-actor. |
| **Mena:** | No fear of him! |
| **Thomasheen:** | He was in this house this evening! |
| **Mena:** | You miss nothing! |
| **Thomasheen:** | You'll have him coming into the house proposin' next! And it might interest you to know that she has been seen on at least one occasion, ducking out of here to meet Scuab after ye were gone to bed. |
| **Mike:** | This is more serious than I thought and 'twill have to stop! I don't want her going the same road as her mother. |
| **Mena:** | Then the old woman must know about it and never told us, which means she is on their side and is probably even encouraging Sive in this. But there's one easy way to stop that sort of thing and that is to move Sive into the west room where I can keep my eye on her and her only means of coming and going will be through our bedroom. |
| **Thomasheen:** | But that alone won't be enough! We must cut out every chance of their meeting. Scuab can still meet her and she comin' and goin' to school, so she must finish with her schoolin'. You can say you're no longer able to manage all the work by yourself, that you need her help, else … |
| **Mena:** | There is no fear of him, I tell you! |
| **Mike:** | You're right, there is no fear of him. He will keep far away from here. But you will have a hard job with Sive. |
| **Thomasheen:** | Will you listen to him cnabshealing again? He's never happy unless 'tis grumbling he is. Wouldn't you have the good word, anyway? You'd swear, to hear you talk, that we were all rogues and thieves. What are we trying to do only make an honest shilling. 'Tisn't |

going around stealing the dead out of their graves we are. 'Twould be a black day for us if we robbed a widow or stole a poor-box from the chapel. Isn't it only bringing two people together in wedlock we are?

**Mena:** When will he give the money?

**Thomasheen:** Seán Dóta is only the half of a fool, not a full one! When the knot is tied, and not before. I have the night wasted in talking with ye. The cocks will be crowing by the time I'm home. [*He goes towards door and turns with his hand on the latch.*] A warning! [*He cocks his thumb towards the old woman's room.*] Watch the oul' one up there! She have the makin's of trouble.

[*Exit* THOMASHEEN SEÁN RUA. MIKE *rises, takes a cup from the dresser and goes to the tankard. He takes off the cover and dips the cup; withdrawing it, he drinks with relish.*]

**Mena:** I would have made tea for you!

**Mike:** Tea is scarce enough without wasting it this hour of the night. [*He replaces the cup, stretches his hands and yawns. He scratches his head roughly.*] I have an early start in the morning and a hard day before me tomorrow. I think I'll go to the bed.

**Mena:** Will you not wait for Sive?

**Mike:** She will be all right. What can harm her? I have no heart somehow for looking her in the face.

**Mena:** I think I could sleep myself. [*She arranges the fire with tongs while* MIKE *unlaces and removes his boots.*]

**Mike:** Would my mother have mind, do you think, for tea?

**Mena:** There is no fear of her! Hasn't she her pipe?

[MENA *loosens her hair, goes to the lamp, and lowers the wick. She turns and exits by the door at side of hearth.* MIKE *places his boots under the working-table and in his socks crosses the kitchen and exits by the same door.*

*The kitchen is empty, eerie-looking in the bad light.*

*The door of the old woman's room opens and she enters the kitchen. She tiptoes to the door of her son's room and listens for a moment. Satisfied, she*

**40**

*turns away and raises the wick of the lamp. She then sits at her place by the fire. She takes the tongs and re-makes the fire. With a look around her she unearths her pipe and thrusts it into her mouth. She finds matches and lights up. She sits thus for a moment or two.*

*Suddenly the door opens and* SIVE *enters. She leans against closed door and holds her hands to her breast, breathing heavily.*]

**Nanna:** Where were you until this hour of the night?

**Sive:** [*Unties her head scarf.*] Down the bohareen at Seamus Dónal's for the loan of a rail for Uncle Mike … That old man, Seán Dóta! Oh! [*She shakes her head and covers her face with her hands.*]

**Nanna:** [*Querulously:*] Seán Dóta?

**Sive:** [*In disgust and fright.*] He was on the road down with me. When we passed by the cumar near Dónal's he made a drive at me! He nearly tore the coat off me. I ran into Dónal's kitchen but he made no attempt to follow. Oh, the way he laughs [*in disgust*], like an ould sick thing. What is the meaning of it all, Gran?

**Nanna:** [*Draws upon her pipe,* SIVE *sits near her.*] 'Tis the nature of the man, child, no more! You will find that men are that way. Being old doesn't change them. It's nothing!

**Sive:** He frightened the life out of me. I never expected it! [*Pause.*] You know, I think, Gran, it was a plan by them … but it's so hard to believe.

**Nanna:** It have the appearance of a plan … Do you know what I think … there are queer doin's goin' on between Mena and Thomasheen Rua.

[MENA *emerges from her room wearing a long nightdress reaching to her toes almost. The two start when they see her.*]

**Mena:** [*Crossly, loudly:*] Are ye going to be there for the night gossiping! A nice thing for the nuns to learn about! Get away to bed out of that! Wasting oil, ye are. Go on! Clear away!

41

[SIVE *and* NANNA *rise.* SIVE *hurries to her room.* NANNA, *concealing the pipe in her palm, follows slowly, and casts a defiant look at* MENA. *Exit* NANNA *and* SIVE. MENA *rakes the fire again and quenches the lamp altogether.*]


**CURTAIN**

# SCENE 3

[*A week later; late afternoon.* NANNA *is at her usual place,* MENA *is kneading dough to make bread on the large table. A large jug of sour milk and a saucer of flour stand there.* MENA *lifts the dough and sprinkles flour on the board. She goes to flour bag, refills the saucer with flour and returns to the table. She continues with the kneading, dusting the sodden bulk of it at times with flour. She turns her head towards the old woman.*]

**Mena:**      Is the pot ready?

[NANNA *looks at a circular flat-bottomed pot near the fire.*]

**Mena:**      Is the hearing going by you, on top of everything else? Or is it how you're trying to rise the temper in me?

**Nanna:**      'Tis aisy enough to do that! The pot is as hot as ever 'twill be.

**Mena:**      And why wouldn't you say so? Sitting there, in the way of everyone!

**Nanna:**      Make your bread, woman! 'Tis hard enough to eat it without having to watch you baking it as well. 'Tis hard enough for a lonely old woman without a child to rock in the cradle.

**Mena:**      Ah, the back o' my hand to you for an oul' hag! There is no good in you – alluding and criticising always. Children bring nothing but misfortune. Didn't you see your own – the good end they came to. The gall of you, condemning me for my lack of child.

[MENA *kneads the dough vigorously, smooths it in a circle, takes a knife from the cupboard and makes a cross on the top of the loaf. Taking a fist of flour she goes to the hearth and sprinkles the bottom of the pot. She returns to the table, takes the dough in her hands and places it in the pot. She takes the tongs and pushing the pot nearer the fire, arranges coals around it. She takes a cloth from the cupboard and cleans the table.*]

**Mena:**      Keep an eye to the bread. I'm going out to give hay to the cows.

43

| | |
|---|---|
| **Nanna:** | [*Pointedly:*] Are you sure it is the cows you are going to see? Are you sure it isn't making mischief you're going? |
| **Mena:** | [*Crossly:*] What is behind that? |
| **Nanna:** | Well enough you know what is behind it. |
| **Mena:** | Come out with what you have to say. Don't be going around in circles like a salmon in a pool. |
| **Nanna:** | Fine words! |
| **Mena:** | Is it how you're so twisted inside of you that you must have the double meaning the whole time? |
| **Nanna:** | I will have what meaning I like! God gave me my tongue, not you! |
| **Mena:** | Now when you are meaning me, will you have strange meanings. What is behind your words? |
| **Nanna:** | That the heart might wither up in your breast – you know what is behind my words. What is the secrecy between yourself and Thomasheen Seán Rua? What is bringing the old man, Seán Dóta, here, day in day out? Will you have the gall to answer? |
| **Mena:** | [*Indignant:*] What has it to do with you? |
| **Nanna:** | It is my grand-daughter that is concerned. |
| **Mena:** | [*Throws back her head and scoffs.*] Your grand-daughter … and do you know, old woman, who her father is? Maybe you will tell? Thanking me from her heart, she should be, the fine match I am making for her. Putting myself out to place her in a gentleman's house. |
| **Nanna:** | Suiting yourself you are, like you always did. |
| **Mena:** | [*Viciously:*] Go to hell! |

[*There is a knock on the door.*]

| | |
|---|---|
| **Mena:** | Come in, let you! |

[*Enter* THOMASHEEN SEÁN RUA. *He gives the customary furtive glance around the kitchen, his eyes coming to rest on the old woman.*

44

MENA *nods encouragingly to him and he advances, leaving door open behind him.*]

**Nanna:** Was there no door in the last house you were in?

**Thomasheen:** [*Carrying an ashplant, hoists it dexterously in his hand.*] The deaf ear is the only cure for your equals ... [*Then, to* MENA:] You will have company shortly, I am thinking. [*Goes to door, looks out to his right and turns again.*]

**Mena:** Who is on the road?

**Thomasheen:** Father and son, but brothers likewise, since the pair of them are sons of the devil.

**Mena:** Who is that?

**Thomasheen:** Two tinker-men ... Pats Bocock and his son, Carthalawn. Two robbers who have no liking for me or any of mine.

**Nanna:** Dacent poor people with no home of their own. Good friends when they are needed.

**Thomasheen:** You know your own! But I know them as rogues! They would cut my gad because I have great call at the matchmaking.

**Nanna:** I would be proud to own them. [*Eyes* MENA *coldly.*] They are visiting here with many a year.

**Mena:** With the hands out and the mouths open, by them. Nothing more and nothing less than beggars.

**Nanna:** They are the people of the road – travelling people. They are above the class beggar.

[*In the distance is the sound of a bodhrán and a voice singing. The sound increases while the occupants of the kitchen await* PATS BOCOCK *and* CARTHALAWN.

*The air of the song is that of* 'Neath the Bright Silvery Light of the Moon – *the Irish ballad not to be confused with* By the Light of the Silvery Moon, *the American ballad. The words of the song are impromptu and created by* CARTHALAWN. (*NB – the same air will persist in all his songs throughout the remainder of the play.*)

*Enter* CARTHALAWN *and* PATS BOCOCK. *They keep step with each other.* PATS *is dressed in an ancient swallow-tail coat and ancient trousers with strong boots. His hat is normal but the hollow in the crown is pushed upwards to give it the gaudy appearance of a top hat. He carries a stout blackthorn stick which he taps on the floor with each step. His left leg is shorter than his right and he walks with a lop-sided motion. He is of stern appearance but looks poverty-stricken nevertheless.*

*His son,* CARTHALAWN, *wears a short coat and is otherwise dressed as his father. In short, his dress is typical of the southern tinker who never wears a collar and tie, who has a jaunty air of good health about him but is above all hard of face. He carries a small bodhrán.*

*What is important about the pair is that both of them keep the same step like soldiers on the march, and have an understanding between each other.*

*Entering the kitchen both men come to a halt before the large table.* PATS *strikes the floor with his stick and taking up the rhythm* CARTHALAWN *taps the bodhrán with his knuckles.*

*He strikes loudly at first, then gently with a very low rubbing of knuckles, preparatory to singing.*

NANNA *rises to her feet, as is the custom when travelling minstrels enter a house, because the first song must be in praise of the man of the house, who is generally absent at work in the fields.*

*As the sound of the bodhrán decreases, the tapping of* PATS' *stick becomes stronger. Then suddenly the tapping of stick and sound of bodhrán become extremely faint and* CARTHALAWN *begins his song. His voice is bell-like in tone. The accent is slightly nasal.*]

**Carthalawn:**    [*Singing:*] Oh! Mike Glavin, you're the man;
               You was always in the van;
               With a dacent house to old man and gorsoon;
               May white snuff be at your wake,
               Bakers bread and curran-y cake
               And plinty on your table, late and soon.

[NANNA *applauds the song, while* MENA *and* THOMASHEEN *are indifferent.* PATS *advances and shakes hands with* NANNA.]

**Pats:**       [*Deep voiced and solemn with unsmiling face:*] 'Tis not aisy, a-girl, to kill you! You have the appearance of a small one, a young one. We do be praying for you in our prayers, whenever we get the notion to kneel. [*He turns to* Mena.] God bless you, bean a' tighe, with your fine appearance and your name for generosity.

[Pats *shakes hands with* Mena. *Her reaction is dismal and suspicious.* Pats *ignores her indifference and extends his hand to* Thomasheen *who turns his back to* Pats.]

**Nanna:** [*In a loud voice, full of warning:*] You are as well off, Pats, without the paw of the devil burning your palm.

[Pats *returns to his son's side; both stand rigid.*]

**Mena:** What is it ye want?

**Pats:** No more than a dorn of sugar and a dusteen of tea. We have the caravan beyant in the steamrolled road. Liam Scuab [*he bends his head in thanks while* Carthalawn *stands rigid*], a dacent man, gave us the side of a loaf. We have our own accoutrements. If there is the giving of tea and sugar we will thank the hand that gives it. If there is not, maybe there is the giving of a silver piece. Is there anything from Thomasheen Seán Rua of the mountain – making it in plenty he is.

[Pats *extends his palm to* Thomasheen *who has turned again to face him.*]

**Thomasheen:** [*Slightly panicky:*] Where would the likes of me come by silver money? There is the half of the country looking for men to work in the bogs. Why should a man beg when there is work before and after him?

**Nanna:** There is no luck in refusing a man of the road!

[Pats *looks with hard eyes at* Thomasheen, *who surveys him with superiority, both hands held behind back.* Pats *opens his mouth and throws back his head in a dangerous fashion. Tapping his stick on the floor, he makes a circuit of the table to where* Carthalawn *stands. He stands by his son's side still tapping.*]

**Pats:** Carthalawn!

[Carthalawn *turns towards his father, a wild look in his eyes.*]

Your best! Your mighty best!

[*Violently* PATS *begins to tap his stick upon the floor.* CARTHALAWN *looks upward at the ceiling and begins to tap the bodhrán with clenched knuckles. For a moment there is loud timing of stickbeat and bodhrán. Then the sound dwindles and* CARTHALAWN *takes up the beat to his usual air, while the stick is pointed at* THOMASHEEN.]

**Carthalawn:** [*Still at 'attention', addresses himself to* THOMASHEEN *while his father stands at 'attention'.*]

May the snails devour his corpse,
And the rain do harm worse;
May the devil sweep the hairy creature soon;
He's as greedy as a sow;
And the crow behind the plough;
That black man from the mountain, Seánín Rua!

[PATS *stamps both his legs and his stick with delight.* NANNA *crows with aged laughter.* THOMASHEEN *turns his back again, boiling with impotent rage.* CARTHALAWN, *having fulfilled his duty, stands unsmiling.*]

**Nanna:** I will give ye the grain o' tay and sugar out of respect to yeer singing.

[MENA *immediately goes and takes her stand between* NANNA *and the dresser.*]

**Mena:** [*Like a guard at arms.*] You will give nothing! Is it how you think that tea and sugar are made by wishing?

**Thomasheen:** [*Turning around viciously:*] Arrah, that's right! Give nothin'! [*Pronounced 'Notten'.*] Give nothin'!! [*He cranes his neck forward.*] The smart men o' the roads. Goin' around criticisin' dacent men an' women. [THOMASHEEN *advances a step, assured of* MENA'*s help.*] Tea and sugar, how are you? The cheek of the two biggest robbers walking the roads of Ireland.

[PATS *and* CARTHALAWN *back towards the door, fearful of their grounds.* THOMASHEEN, *thinking he has gained the ascendancy, follows up his victory.* PATS *and* CARTHALAWN *stand in line with the door.*]

**Thomasheen:**   [*Confident:*] Will ye look at the appearance of them! A short leg and a half-fool! Two with the one word, goin' around with their songs, frightenin' half the country. Go on away to yeer smelly caravan and not be disgustin' respectable people!

[THOMASHEEN *draws back his right hand as if to strike them. As he does so,* PATS *taps again with his stick.* CARTHALAWN *knuckles the bodhrán. Both assume ritual dignity to the rhythm of bodhrán and blackthorn.*]

**Pats:**   [*To* CARTHALAWN:] Carthalawn, your best! Your Almighty best!

[*With temper he keeps tapping. Imperiously he points stick at* THOMASHEEN *as in a ritual from time immemorial.* CARTHALAWN *sings slowly, his voice bell-like and piercing. The tapping and the bodhrán grow quieter.*]

**Carthalawn:**   [*Sings:*] On the road from Abbeyfeale,
Sure I met a man with meal,
Come here, said he, and pass your idle time;
On me he made quite bold
Saying the young will wed the old
And the old man have the money for the child.

[THOMASHEEN *turns to look to* MENA *who stands helpless.* PATS *taps his stick loudly on the floor with appreciation, full of smiles and headshaking.* NANNA *crows with delight simultaneously.* THOMASHEEN *returns to where* MENA *stands barring* NANNA's *way to the dresser.* MENA *folding her hands over her bosom in a fighting attitude, advances until she faces* CARTHALAWN *and his father.*]

**Mena:**   You brought your story well! [*To* PATS:] Come out with what you have to say. Don't be hiding behind the words of a half-fool [*indicating* CARTHALAWN].

**Pats:**   'Tis the talk of the country that Seán Dóta the farmer is marrying a young girl out of this house. If their tales are true her name is Sive. The people are saying that it is a strange match that a young girl who is at the start of her days should marry an old man who is at the end of his. They say he is struggling to keep the

49

spark of life inside of him. They say she is the flower of the parish.

**Mena:** How dare you cast your aspersions under this roof.

**Pats:** [*Calmly:*] 'Tis only what the people are saying! [*He points his stick at* THOMASHEEN.] They say he is the man who brought it about; that he will score well out of it. This only what the people are saying [*roguishly*]. That is the common word everywhere our feet take us.

**Mena:** And what is it to them or to you either, the way we conduct ourselves? Is it the first time a young girl marries a man older than her? She is matching well for herself.

**Pats:** There is no one saying otherwise.

**Nanna:** The devil's work, that's what it is!

**Pats:** We will come calling the night of the wedding.

**Thomasheen:** There will be nothing here for ye.

**Pats:** We will come all the same, welcome or not!

**Nanna:** There was always welcome here for Pats Bocock.

**Pats:** 'Tis the changing of the times.

**Thomasheen:** [*To* PATS:] 'Twill be a good change when the likes of ye do a day's work. Into jail ye should be put, a brace of dirty beggars.

**Pats:** [*Full of venom:*] I'm listening to you, Thomasheen Seán Rua and I'm watching you and I'm telling you what you are. You are the bladder of a pig, the snout of a sow; you are the leavings of a hound, the sting of a wasp. You will die roaring. Carthalawn! Your best! Your almighty best!

[PATS *stands rigid and taps the stick.* CARTHALAWN *knuckles the bodhrán, the volume is reduced and* CARTHALAWN *sings as both men turn for the door in step.*]

50

**Carthalawn:** [*Singing:*] May the snails devour his corpse,
And the rain do harm worse;
May the devil sweep the hairy creature soon;

[*They go out, but the singing is heard, growing fainter.*]

He's as greedy as a sow;
And the crow behind the plough;
That black man from the mountain, Seánín Rua!

[THOMASHEEN *goes to the door and closes it after* PATS *and* CARTHALAWN. *Flexing the stick with his hands behind his back, he glares at* NANNA.]

**Thomasheen:** Who has been broadcasting my private affairs around the countryside. [*With* NANNA *alone he is confident again and bent upon cowarding her.*] You are a lone woman with your husband feeding worms in his trench. You have terrible gumption with no one left to back you.

**Mena:** Go on, you oul' wretch ... Answer the man ... Where is your stiffness gone to?

**Thomasheen:** With the county home staring you in the face?

**Mena:** Dependent upon people who work and scrape to make ends meet ...

**Nanna:** Ye had ...

**Thomasheen:** Go on! Say it, you oul' hag! Aaaah! You'll say nothin' now. Face the end of your days, oul' woman!

**Nanna:** Ye had little to say a while back, either of ye, when the composing was going on. I will tell my son when he comes home the way ye are at me.

**Mena:** Little your son cares about you. Long ago you should have been put in your place. Small thanks you show for the freedom you have here. Would it not enter your head that there is many an oul' woman of your age walking the road without a roof above or a bed beneath them.

51

**Thomasheen:** Sure the county home is filled to the jaws with the likes of her. You will see the crowds of them sticking their heads out of the windows watching the visitors coming and going and they hoping that someone will come to take them away out of it. 'Tis the sport of Cork to see the way they do be haggling and scraping over the few potatoes and the forkful of meat. [*Solemnly:*] Ah, but sure the hardest of all, God pity us, is that they will stop the oul' women of smoking. An oul' lady from the other side of the mountain that used to have a liking for her pipe of tobaccy went out of her mind after three days. She could be heard screeching in the other world. They had a piece of sacking over her mouth to keep her quiet but sure that was no good but as little. She started scraping herself till the flesh hung from her in gibbles and the blood used to be coursin' down out of her in streams. 'Twas a madness for the pipe, you see! [*Sanctimoniously:*] She was a terrible sight when she died. They buried her in the middle of the night with not a living Christian in the world of her own people to say a prayer for her … Aah! Some people do not know when they are well off!

**Mena:** She will change!

**Thomasheen:** She have the appearance of one that won't!

**Mena:** She'll change! She's enough of a burden without becoming a curse altogether.

**Thomasheen:** Walking the road she should be like the rest of her equals.

**Mena:** Will she walk the road? … Far from it … Where is the independent woman we had in her? [MENA *lifts the latch and opens the door. She indicates the world beyond with a flourish.*] Go on, if you have the mind for it! [*Shouts:*] Go on and put your bag on your back and go begging from door to door. Will she go, do

52

you think? … will she? … No! nor go! What a fool she would be to leave her warm fire with the pipe handy by her and the good table with her three rounds of diet every day.

**Nanna:**  [*To the fire:*] There is a hatchery of sin in this house.

[*Her voice is full of defeat.* MENA *bounces forward till she is close to* NANNA. THOMASHEEN *advances likewise.*]

**Mena:**  [*Violently:*] No more of your sharp answers, you oul' wretch. You sit there, day in, day out, taking all you can get without a word of thanks. You will have a puss by you like the child in the cot feeding yourself up with the fruits of our labours, taking all as if you were born for it, like the queen of the land.

**Nanna:**  [*Repeats:*] 'Like a child in the cradle'. [*Shakes her head pitifully.*]

**Mena:**  [*Stiffens with rage.*] Is it my fault that your son is a tired gomeril of a man?

**Nanna:**  A cluckin' hen won't hatch!

**Mena:**  [*Advances and draws back her hand.*] I will strike you. [*Full of venom:*] I will take the head from your shoulders.

[MENA *draws back her hand again to strike a blow.* THOMASHEEN *drops his stick, intervenes promptly, and drags* MENA *back towards the door, she struggles in his grasp, to have at* NANNA, *but he holds her firmly.*]

**Thomasheen:**  [*From behind* MENA, *still holding her, to* NANNA:] See what you are after doing? [*Guilefully:*] You have upset her. [*To* NANNA:] You will answer for your evil soul.

**Mena:**  She'll burn! She'll burn the day she gives over her life!

**Thomasheen:**  [*To* NANNA:] Don't be goadin' her! Don't be goadin' her.

**Nanna:**  [*Having crossed to her bedroom door,* NANNA *turns.*] I'll say it again. There's a hatchery of sin in this house.

[*When she has gone,* Thomasheen *releases his hold on* Mena *who looks with murderous intent towards the room into which* Nanna *has entered.*]

Thomasheen: Leave her be for the now. The mind for fight is gone from her. [*He stoops, and retrieves his stick, and makes small circles on the floor with its point.*] There is a play to all things. D'you see the oul' cock salmon that do be hidin' in the deep hole of the river. They will be firing stones at him and making plans for his capture. They will be poisoning and making the use of nets but they might as well be idle. [*Is very positive:*] 'Tis the age that will do the work. 'Tis the mounting up of the years. Aaah! age is a killin's thief! Age is the boy that will stand no nonsense. He have a grip like a double-knot ... The old woman is tiring.

[*Pause.*]

Mena: When will he give the money?

Thomasheen: If there is a wedding, 'twill be on the morning of the wedding, on the word of a man. Is there any word out of the girl?

Mena: She will do what is to be done. Am I to be telling you forever?

Thomasheen: But have she said the word out of her mouth?

Mena: What is the need for that?

Thomasheen: It would put my mind more at ease.

Mena: Well, you can rest your mind. She will marry Seán Dóta and that will be the end of it.

Thomasheen: 'Tis a fine thing to hear the good word anyway. Still I may tell you I will not rest happy till he has the halter on her.

Mena: [*Raises a hand to* Thomasheen *to ensure silence – she listens a moment.*] That will be Sive now. When she comes in, pass her the time of day – no more; then go away about

54

your business and leave the rest in my hands. 'Tis work for a woman now.

**Thomasheen:** [*Hurries to window and looks out.*] You will put the best things before her.

**Mena:** Gather yourself and be ready to go.

**Thomasheen:** What about? … [*He points to* NANNA's *room.*]

**Mena:** She'll dance to my tune … Aisy!

[*The latch lifts and* SIVE *enters. She is dressed as before and carries the satchel of books in her hand. She looks from* MENA *to* THOMASHEEN, *frowns for the barest fraction of a second, and lays her satchel on the table. She undoes her headscarf and lays it across the satchel.*]

**Thomasheen:** [*Sweetly:*] Is the schoolin' over for today with ye?

**Sive:** [*To* MENA:] The bicycle got punctured again. I had to walk from beyond the cross.

**Thomasheen:** I will have to be going. There is a great length coming to the days, thanks be to God. We will have the summer now down on the door before we know.

**Mena:** Goodbye to you, Thomasheen.

**Thomasheen:** [*Nods politely to* SIVE, *who edges away to let him pass.*] I will be seeing ye again, please God, before we're older.

**Mena:** [*Impatiently:*] We will be here! [*Inclination of her head.*]

[THOMASHEEN *twirls his stick and opens the door.*]

**Thomasheen:** [*Airily:*] Good luck, all.

[*When he has gone,* MENA *takes one of the buckets from under working-table and pours water from the drinking pail into it. She replaces the drinking pail.* MENA *then scoops several fistfuls of meal from the bag into the bucket.*]

**Sive:** [*Hesitant:*] The tubes of the bicycle are full of holes.

[MENA *dries her hands on her apron and turns to* SIVE.]

**Mena:** [*Sympathetically:*] We will have to do something about it, for sure. I will tell himself to be on the look for a pair of new tubes in the village. Will I wet a mouthful o' tea for you while you're waiting for the dinner. [SIVE *is too surprised to reply.*] There is a piece of sweet cake I have put away. You must be tired after your day.

Sive:        [*Befuddled:*] No ... no ... don't bother with the tea! I'll wait until the dinner.

Mena:     A cup of milk, so! [*Without waiting for reply, she hurries to dresser, takes a cup, fills it and forces it on* SIVE.] It must be an ease for you to get away from the nuns and the books, but sure we won't have much more of the schooling now.

[*Gently* MENA *forces* SIVE *to a chair near the table.* SIVE *places the cup before her and looks bewilderedly at* MENA *at the word 'school'.*]

Mena:     Any of the girls in the parish would give their right hand to have the chance that's before you.

Sive:        But ...

Mena:     [*Quickly before* SIVE *can reply:*] Don't think about it now. Think of the handling of thousands and the fine clothes and perfumery. Think of the hundreds of pounds in creamery cheques that will come in the door to you and the servant boy and the servant girl falling all over you for fear you might dirty your hands with work.

Sive:        [*Shakes her head several times as though to ward off* MENA*'s words.*] You don't know ... you ... you ...

Mena:     Sit down now and rest yourself. You could have your grandmother with you. Think of the joy it would give the poor woman to have the run of such a fine house ... and to see you settled there. 'Tis a fine thing for you, my girl and sure, what matter if he's a few years older than you. Won't we be all old in a handful of short years? Ah! I would give my right hand to be in your shoes.

**Sive:** [*Shakes her head continually.*] Please, please … you don't know what you are saying. How can you ask me such a thing?

**Mena:** Now, tomorrow himself will call to the convent and tell the reverend mother that you will not be going in any more. What would a grown-up woman like you want with spending your days in the middle of children.

**Sive:** I could never live with that old man. [*Entreats* MENA:] Fancy the thought of waking in the light of day and looking at him with the small head of him. Oh, my God! No! I could never! … I could not even think of it!

**Mena:** [*Still motherly:*] Nonsense, child! That is nothing. Have sense for yourself. I know what you are going into. Do you think I would not gainsay him if it wasn't the best thing for you. [*Places a hand around* SIVE*'s shoulder.*] Sit here, child, and drink your milk.

[MENA *gently brings* SIVE *to the chair, seats her and stands behind her with both hands resting lightly on* SIVE*'s shoulders.* MENA*'s face becomes shrewd.* SIVE *looks vacantly before her – towards the audience.*]

**Mena:** Will you picture yourself off to the chapel every Sunday in your motor car with your head in the air and you giving an odd look out of the window at the poor oinsheachs in their donkey-and-cars and their dirty oul' shawls and their faces yellow with the dirt by them. Will you thank God that you won't be for the rest of your days working for the bare bite and sup like the poor women of these parts.

**Sive:** [*Raises her head and entwines her hands.*] Imagine what the girls at school would say! Imagine going to a dance with him, or going up the chapel with him!

**Mena:** All I know is that you will be independent. You will have no enemy when you have the name of money.

57

**Sive:**     I don't know what to think or to say. I do not want to give offence, but I will never marry such a man. I will not marry at all!

**Mena:**     [*Motherly again:*] You will change! You will change when you think by yourself of the misery you are leaving; when you think of the way you were born.

[SIVE *eagerly turns and looks innocently at* MENA. *She is changed suddenly to an eager girl awaiting the solution of a problem that has for a long time baffled her.*]

**Sive:**     Surely you don't remember when I was born. [*Her eyes widen as she looks at* MENA. *For the first time she takes an interest in* MENA's *soliloquy.*] Nobody ever told me about my father or mother or what sort of people they were.

[SIVE *looks into* MENA's *face searching for the truth.*]

**Mena:**     I will tell the tale. Himself would never bring himself to say it. You would think it was some kind of a blemish that should be hidden and sure, what was it, only the work of nature. Your mother, God grant her a bed in heaven, was a nice lie of a girl. Your father took himself away quickly out of these parts and, if he is alive, never made himself known. There was no blame to your mother, God help her. Your grandmother, for all yeer talking and whispering behind my back, was never the one to come out with the truth.

**Sive:**     But my father ... wasn't he drowned in England?

**Mena:**     Your father was never a father, God forgive him. He straightened his sails and disappeared like the mist of a May morning. It was no wonder your mother died with the shame of it. No blame, achree! [*With feeling then:*] No blame to what is mortal. Do you think it is how two people will stay apart forever who have blood becoming a flood in their veins. It is the way things happen ... [*conviction*] ... the sound of fiddles playing airy hornpipes, the light of a moon on the pale face of a river, the whispered word ... the meeting of soft arms and strong arms ... [*pauses.*]

**Sive:** I thought you said you'd tell me about my father.

**Mena:** [*Unaccountably vexed:*] I'm telling you your father was nothing. He was no father. He had no name. You have no name. You will have no name till you take a husband. Do you see the hungry greyhound or the mongrel dog? It is the same way with a man. It is no more than the hunger. It is time you were told, my girl. You are a bye-child, a common bye-child – a bastard!

[SIVE *attempts to rise.* MENA *roughly pushes her back in the chair.*]

**Mena:** You will sleep with that old woman no longer. [*She flings the schoolbag across the room.*] There will be no more school for you. School is a place for schoolmasters and children. Every woman will come to the age when she will have a mind for a room of her own. I mind when I was a child, *when I was a woman*, there were four sisters of us in the one room. There was no corner of a bed we could call our own. We used to sit into the night talking and thieving and wondering where the next ha'penny would come from or thinking would it ever come to our turn to meet a boy that we might go with, and be talking with and maybe make a husband out of. We would kill [*vexed*]. We would beg, borrow or steal. We would fire embers of fire at the devil to leave the misery of our own house behind us, to make a home with a man, any man that would show four walls to us for his time in the world. [*In a voice of warning:*] Take no note of the man who has nothing to show for himself, who will be full of rameish and blather, who would put wings on ould cows for you but has no place to make a marriage bed for you. Take heed of a man with a piece of property. He will stand over his promise. He will keep the good word for you because he has the keeping of words ... Now go to the room and be sure to think of what I said.

59

[SIVE *rises instinctively goes towards her own room but remembering, turns and exits by the far door to* MENA'S *bedroom.*]

## END OF ACT ONE

# ACT TWO

## SCENE 1

[MENA *sits at the table preparing the shopping list for the wedding. There is a knock on the door.*]

**Mena:** [*Listens a moment.*] Come in!

[*Enter* LIAM SCUAB. *He looks around the kitchen.*]

**Mena:** You have the devil's own gall coming here. Lucky for you that Mike is away.

**Liam:** I don't give a hatful of bornacks for Mike or for you either. I come here to see Sive.

**Mena:** What do you want Sive for?

**Liam:** I want to talk with her.

**Mena:** You put a journey on yourself for nothing. Sive isn't here. [*Turning away to re-arrange fire.*]

**Liam:** How is it her bike is up against the wall of the house?

**Mena:** [*Angry:*] Are you telling me she's here? Are you making a liar out of me in my own house?

**Liam:** I didn't call you a liar. I only thought you might be making a mistake.

**Mena:** [*Loudly:*] Same thing, isn't it? Didn't I say she wasn't here?

**Liam:** There's no harm if I wait for her so. I won't be in your way.

**Mena:** You have no business here. If Mike finds you there will be war. You're not wanted in this house. Clear off on your road and don't be vexing me.

| Liam: | I have no wish to make an enemy out of you. I will wait till she comes. |
|---|---|
| Mena: | [*Violently:*] Will you have your own way in all things, will you? Will you be coming into people's houses causing trouble. Get away out of here or I'll get the tongs to you. |
| Liam: | I love her! |
| Mena: | [*Mimicking:*] You love her! You do! You love her! You gomaill. |

[*There is a sound without, and* MIKE *enters.*]

| Mena: | Look, what's before you! Look at him and don't blame me, because he wouldn't go for me. |
|---|---|
| Mike: | [*In overcoat with cap, places sack and whip aside and throws cap on table.*] I see him! [MIKE *sits on the sacks.*] |
| Liam: | I mean no harm, Mike Glavin, to you or your wife. |
| Mike: | [*Taking off his boots.*] What do you want, Scuab? |
| Liam: | I want to see Sive. |
| Mike: | [*Mutters thoughtfully:*] You came to see Sive, did you? Sive, faith, of all ones! What do you want to see her for, Scuab? |
| Liam: | To have a talk with her. |
| Mike: | [*Calmly:*] No, you'll have no talk with her. |
| Liam: | Only for a moment. |
| Mike: | She's in my care. You'll have to talk with me. |
| Liam: | I know you won't heed me but I was told that Sive was getting married. |
| Mike: | Who told you that? |
| Liam: | The two tinkers, Carthalawn and Pats Bocock. They were singing a song. It was easy to read the news. |
| Mena: | Now for sure you're a fool, when you pay attention to the grunting of pigs. |

| | |
|---|---|
| **Liam:** | They make sense in their own way. |
| **Mike:** | 'Tis nonsense. |
| **Liam:** | If it is nonsense, so, tell me why is Thomasheen Seán Rua, the matchmaker, coming here every day and often twice in the day? |
| **Mike:** | He has how own business with me. You're like a magistrate with your foxy digs at us. |
| **Liam:** | All right, so, but what is the reason for another thing? |
| **Mike:** | What other thing? |
| **Liam:** | The old man, Seán Dóta, the farmer, he is coming here every day now too. |
| **Mike:** | Is he now, and what do you make out of it all? |
| **Liam:** | I have heard him talking to himself on the road. |
| **Mena:** | Talking to himself, will you tell us? |
| **Liam:** | I have heard him. |
| **Mena:** | And what does he be saying? |
| **Liam:** | Things about Sive, and how he will warm her before she is much older. A lot of other things, too, but most of it not fit to mention again. |
| **Mike:** | [*Crossly:*] So what if he does? What is it to you? |
| **Liam:** | I know he will marry Sive. |

[MIKE *and* MENA *exchange shrewd looks.*]

| | |
|---|---|
| **Mike:** | Ah, yerra, you're going farther from sense with every word. |
| **Mena:** | Sure, isn't that what I told him. |
| **Liam:** | It's hard to believe it could be true. |
| **Mike:** | There is no truth at all to it, man. |
| **Liam:** | Oh, for God's sake, will the two of you stop treating me like a child. The whole parish knows what's going on. It is the talk at every crossroads that Sive |

63

is matchmaking with Seán Dóta. In the village the public-houses are full with the mockery of it.

**Mike:** [*Advancing a step.*] I've come to the last sod with you, Scuab. Get out of this house before I be tempted to take a weapon in my hands. [*Clenches his fists.*] You'd better be going, Scuab, or I'll take the whip to you.

**Mena:** And I the tongs. I'll put streaks on you worse than a raddle-stick.

**Liam:** [*Pleads:*] In the honour of God, I beseech you to forget about violence. I tell you I want no trouble. If I have upset ye, I'm sorry, but surely if ye know God ye must think of this terrible auction. Ye must know that a day will dawn for all of us when an account must be given. Do not think of me. I promise I will leave these parts till Sive is a woman. I swear that on my dead mother. But do not give her to that rotting old man with his gloating eyes and trembling hands.

**Mike:** [*Less angrily:*] Enough, Scuab! Go! [*Turns aside.*]

**Mena:** Wasn't it one of your breed that blackened her mother's name, wasn't it? Oh, the cheek of you, you upstart out of the gutter.

**Liam:** Think, woman, I beg of you! Think, Mike Glavin! Forget about yourselves and see it with good eyes instead of greedy ones. Have you knowledge of the Crucified Son of God? [*Shakes his head with emotion.*] Are you forgetting Him who died on Calvary? Are you forgetting the sorrow and terrible sadness of His bloody Face as He looks at ye now? Will ye stand and watch each other draw the hard crooked thorns deep into His helpless body?

**Mena:** [*Violent temper.*] Gerraway out-a that! Get away!

**Liam:** [*Backing towards the door.*] Nothing in Heaven or Hell could move ye to see wrong!

[MENA *whips the sharp knife off the dresser.*]

**Mena:**     I'll open you! I'll open you if you vex me more.

**Liam:**     I'm going. You'll live to remember this night.

[*Exit* LIAM. MENA *scowlingly replaces the knife and looks at* MIKE *who stands sullen.*]

**Mena:**     What's wrong with you now?

**Mike:**     Nothing!

**Mena:**     Well, put a stir on yourself. You have a priest to see.

**Mike:**     [*Sighs.*] Aye!

[*Enter* SIVE *looking a little wan.*]

**Sive:**     I thought I heard the voice of Liam Scuab.

**Mena:**     You thought right! He was here.

**Sive:**     What was he looking for?

**Mena:**     He's a strange one! He came wishing you joy. You'd never think he would. He wished you joy and plenty on your wedding.

**Sive:**     [*In astonishment:*] He wished me joy and plenty!

**Mena:**     [*Nods.*] And he'll pray for your happiness and he's going away altogether to foreign places. That is the last we'll see of him, God help us. That the blessing of God go with him!

**Sive:**     [*In wonder:*] Did he say any more?

**Mena:**     [*To* MIKE:] Did he say any more?

**Mike:**     Mmmmm!

**Mena:**     Divil the word more, only to turn on his heel as airy as you please and off with him.

**Sive:**     He's gone for good? [*Turns towards the room.*] To think that he's gone for good.

**Mena:**     Gone, he is!

**Sive:**     [*Tearfully:*] Oh! Liam could never do a thing like that.

*[She turns with her hands to her face and exits.]*

**Mena:** There 'tis all now settled and no more to it.

**Mike:** She has no heart for it.

**Mena:** She'll have heart in time. 'Twill be nothing at all when she gets settled in for herself. What way was I when I came to this house? No one to say a good word for me and amn't I coming into my own now in spite of all?

**Mike:** That was a different story! You were wanting to get married. Sive has no wish for it.

**Mena:** *[Crossly:]* Are you at it again? Cnabshealin'? It was different in no way. How was it different? With an oul' devil in the corner screechin' at me the length of the day and a dirty brat of an orphan bawling in the corner.

**Mike:** Sive is young!

**Mena:** *[Indignantly:]* And wasn't I young?

**Mike:** I know! I know! But ...

**Mena:** But this, and but that! I'm going for a bucket of water to the well. You can eat, if you want it.

**Mike:** I'll shave if I'm to see the priest.

**Mena:** *[Taking a bucket.]* There's water in the kettle for you.

*[Exit MENA.]*

**Mike:** I can eat a bite when I'm done.

*[MIKE takes a brush, soap and an open razor and places them on working-table. He fetches the kettle and pours water into the basin on table, finds a towel in the cupboard and sets about softening his bristle.*

*Enter NANNA silently. She is on her way to her chair by the fire when her movement is arrested by a sudden thought. She turns.]*

**Nanna:** What are you shaving for at this hour of the day? Is it Sunday or Monday we have?

**Mike:** *[Without turning.]* Is it a sin to shave? Must I answer for everything?

**Nanna:** [*Tone of menace.*] You will answer for enough in your own time.

[MIKE *spins around suddenly, holding soap and brush in his hands.*]

**Mike:** And what is this, all of a sudden?

**Nanna:** There is a curse of evil on this house. Your dead sister and my dead daughter will curse it from her grave.

**Mike:** [*Wearily, irritably:*] Will ye never stop pestering me?

**Nanna:** There was never an ounce of luck in this house since that greasy bitch darkened the door of it.

**Mike:** [*Dangerously:*] You mean, who?

**Nanna:** I mean that hungry sow that sleeps with you. I mean that pauperised wretch you call a wife.

**Mike:** You never had a good word for her. She's my wife and she'll always be that. A man's wife will always be his wife, let them both be what they will.

**Nanna:** Far be it from me to spoil your home and put ye fighting. But surely you must give an ear to the word of your own mother that suckled you when you were a tiny boy, that watched over you like a hawk, that kept the wind and the rain away from you. [*Near to tears.*] Surely you will listen to your own mother that loved you as no one ever will.

**Mike:** [*Weary, considerate:*] What ails you, mother … what ails my mother?

**Nanna:** Sive, Mike, Sive! Poor Sive! What are ye doing to her? Is there no heart in you at all?

**Mike:** [*Head averted.*] 'Tis for the best, I tell you. 'Tis for the best.

**Nanna:** 'Tis for the best that she marry an ould fooleen of a man! Mike, you will not look at me in the face and say 'tis for the best! Will you look at me in the face, my son!

| **Mike:** | Are you trying to drive nails into me? What am I to do? Do you want to have *she* be like her poor mother? Don't you know that Scuab has an eye for her? |
|---|---|
| **Nanna:** | Liam Scuab is a good boy. He would make a good husband. There is lies to you, Mike! |
| **Mike:** | Did his cousin make a good husband for Sive's mother? Will you have her conceiving again under sin? Will you have another Scuab do bad work? |
| **Nanna:** | That is a wrong thing to say, leanav! Oh! 'tis a wrong thing. Sive and Liam Scuab will not wear under temptation. There is a sweet thing in their love. Shame to you, Mike! |
| **Mike:** | Will you forget so quick? Quick was Liam Scuab's cousin when he reneged your daughter. Quick was he after his days and nights of pleasure. Quick was my sister's death. Quick is death, mother! [*Losing control.*] Quick, quick, quick is everything. Quick is marriage and quick is love and quick is youth. Quick is Sive's womanhood before we know it. We can't ask all things nice, mother. The nicest of things happen quick, likewise the worst things. Quick is the best thought and thing of a man and gone before he knows it. Sive is lucky. She marries young with nothing to bear. She is only a girl and lucky, not a woman who will have been thinking of men. |
| **Nanna:** | How is it all men will find words to save themselves? [*Sadly:*] Women must pay for all happiness. That is their sorry shape, God help us. |
| **Mike:** | [*Embarrassed:*] Go aisy, mother! |
| **Nanna:** | How can I go aisy when my own grandchild is for sale like an animal. |
| **Mike:** | [*Shouts:*] Am I to have no rest from ye? Are ye to be pricking and prodding always? |

[MIKE *opens the towel and places the soap, razor and brush in it. He folds the towel about them. He opens the front door to the yard. He takes the basin in one hand and the towel in the other, all in a passionate temper.*]

**Mike:** I will shave in the stable. There will be no nagging there!

[*Exit* MIKE. *Slowly* NANNA *rises and closes the door after him. She goes to her own room.*]

## CURTAIN

# SCENE 2

[*A fortnight later; night.* NANNA *is alone. She fills a cup with milk from the tankard and sits close by the fire supping it. She lifts her head when she hears a delicate tapping at the door. The tapping is repeated when she does not answer immediately.*

*Slowly* NANNA *rises and goes to the door. She opens it.*

*Enter* PATS.]

**Pats:** I'm for the past hour at the four sides of the house watching and waiting to know would I see were you alone or was there someone here with you.

**Nanna:** I'm alone now, but I won't be for long. Mike will be from the bog shortly. He should be here now, whatever is keeping him.

**Pats:** 'Tis a good thing you are alone, anyway. [*Looks around.*] And that there's no one to hear or see.

**Nanna:** There's a great air of trickery about you.

**Pats:** I saw the young girl, Sive, and the other one going the road to town airly in the day.

**Nanna:** Gone to buy the wedding clothes they are. £50 Dóta gave to buy the clothes and the drink for the wedding.

**Pats:** 'Tis about the wedding I came. Last night we made a plan in the caravan.

**Nanna:** What good is a plan now with the wedding tomorrow morning? The poor child is nearly out of her mind these past weeks.

**Pats:** At the caravan last night we were boiling a hare, the two of us, when who should arrive but Liam Scuab, that has the notion for Sive. A fine gradhbhar boy he is, and his heart broke for love of the girl. He haven't laid eyes on her this long time.

**Nanna:** They keep her in the house all the time. There's always a one to watch her for fear she'd go out.

**Pats:** We thought of a plan, the three of us. And the plan is for the girl to steal out of the house tonight. He will be waiting for her at his own place.

**Nanna:** They watch her every minute.

**Pats:** After she goes to bed, who will watch her?

**Nanna:** [*Excitedly:*] 'Tis true, and there's a window to the room.

**Pats:** She will go in whatever clothes she will be wearing. Whisht … [*pause.*] Did you hear the sound of a step?

[*Both listen.*]

**Nanna:** 'Twas nothing! What else will she do?

**Pats:** She will go to the young man's house and they will be married as soon as possible.

**Nanna:** 'Twill be a great suck-in for all of them!

**Pats:** Dóta, the farmer, has no business with a young girl. If he have a mind for women let him lie down with his own equals. He have no love for her. 'Tis the flesh of her he do be doting over. The young man have a true heart for her. She have a true heart for him. What more!

**Nanna:** [*Giving him a coin.*] God spare you to the roads you travel, Pats, for last night's work.

**Pats:** 'Twas done willing! God the Master makes His own reward!

**Nanna:** Will they marry for sure in the morning?

**Pats:** They will marry for sure. [*Takes a letter from his pocket.*] When Sive comes from the town, give her this. There is writing inside that will tell her all. Let no one see you or they will rise to the scent. 'Tis the one chance we have.

**Nanna:** [*Takes the letter.*] No one will see, I promise you. May God reward you for your goodness.

71

**Pats:** 'Tis a small thing to do for my sins, and I have them in a plenty.

**Nanna:** It might be the best if you went away now.

**Pats:** There's more to go yet. When the women come from the town I will come again. Carthalawn, my son, will come too. We will sing a song, moryah, and give our blessing to the wedding. They will think that all is well if we pretend to expect the marriage of Dóta and the girl.

**Nanna:** Go now and God speed you!

[*Suddenly* MIKE *appears in the doorway.*]

**Mike:** I saw you coming, Pats Bocock, and I was watching you around the house. Like a spy you were; peeping and ducking like a spy!

[NANNA *hurriedly conceals the letter, noticed by* MIKE.]

**Pats:** I have gone through many a place in my travels, but 'tis the first time I was called a spy.

**Mike:** [*Entering.*] What were you doing, then, around the house? Looking here and there and walking on your toes!

**Pats:** Thinking to steal a few eggs I was, but I changed my mind and said to myself that I would ask first before I went stealing.

**Mike:** No one would refuse you for an egg in this house.

**Pats:** Ah, sure, I know that well, but there is no fun in eating eggs unless they are stolen!

**Mike:** [*Suspicious:*] You're making up, I'm thinkin'! I don't know what thing brought you, but I'd say 'twas nothing good.

**Pats:** I've done you no harm but if I'm not wanted, I'll go.

**Mike:** And I've done you no harm and you were always welcome here and you always will. But come straight

|          |                                                                                       |
| -------- | ------------------------------------------------------------------------------------- |
|          | to the house from the road and there will be a warmer welcome for you. No man likes to have his house watched. |
| **Pats:** | God forbid I should make a watch on a man or his house. A man who will spy upon another man or upon another man's woman is a troubled man. Goodnight to the two of ye and God bless. |
| **Mike:** | And God bless to you! |

[*Exit* PATS.]

|          |                                                                                       |
| -------- | ------------------------------------------------------------------------------------- |
| **Mike:** | What did he want, mother? What was the tinker doing here? |
| **Nanna:** | Must a mother answer to her only son? Is there no respect for old people? |
| **Mike:** | I have always tried to please you. I never gave lip. It is hard to be a good son and a good husband under the same roof. [*Sits down and leans forward, looking into space.*] |
| **Nanna:** | We were happy and content here before that woman came into the house. Where is the love you used to have for Sive? Everywhere you went you used to take her with you. You were better than a father to her. Where is the promise you gave to your sister? |
| **Mike:** | [*Harried:*] Will you not be tormenting me again. Didn't I say to you that a horse can't be guided two roads at once. [*Suspiciously:*] And what is it you were hiding from me when I came in? You expect me to be open with you, while you play trickery with the tinker. Tell me what it was you were hiding? |
| **Nanna:** | I have nothing to hide from you. |
| **Mike:** | There you are now, telling me lies again! |
| **Nanna:** | I'll tell you the truth if you'll promise on your word as my son that 'twill be secret. |
| **Mike:** | I promise on my word as your son! [*Solemnly.*] |

| | |
|---|---|
| **Nanna:** | [*Withdrawing the letter.*] 'Tis a letter from Liam Scuab to Sive. There is no harm in it. Only saying good-bye to her in his own way. 'Tis the kind of notion young people have! Little faldals between them. |
| **Mike:** | Why was Pats Bocock prowling in the yard? |
| **Nanna:** | He was afraid to give the letter to anyone but me. Sure, if your wife or Thomasheen Seán Rua got hold of it, wouldn't they only set fire to it. |
| **Mike:** | Are you sure there's nothing more in it? |
| **Nanna:** | Wouldn't I tell you if there was? |
| **Mike:** | [*Reflectively.*] Mmmmmh! |
| **Nanna:** | And would I be such a fool as to show it to you if there was anything more in it? |
| **Mike:** | That's true, I suppose. |
| **Nanna:** | Mike, my son, I know that in your own heart you're against this match. I know you do be thinking your own thoughts about it, about that little wraneen of a man and your sister's child that you love. |
| **Mike:** | Mother, will you leave me alone! Ye'll see me out of my mind between all of ye. |
| **Nanna:** | Give her this letter yourself, Mike. |
| **Mike:** | Oh, no! |
| **Nanna:** | She will never get it so, because they will be watching for me to leave my room and they would see me giving it to her. |
| **Mike:** | I … I … I can't, mother! [*Dread sincerity.*] |
| **Nanna:** | 'Twill be the last bit of comfort or consolation she'll have from this night to her grave. |
| **Mike:** | Good God! Why are ye all at me! |
| **Nanna:** | If you have a bit of love left in you for Sive and me, you will take this letter and give it to her. What harm will it do? Sure, there's nothing inside in it |

74

only a last goodbye and wishing her joy for her wedding.

**Mike:** Mother, I would do anything in my power, but …

**Nanna:** Then do this small thing I ask you. No one will know and you will bring joy to your mother's heart and maybe a small bit of joy for Sive.

**Mike:** Give me the letter!

**Nanna:** [*Handing the letter to him.*] God bless you, my son.

**Mike:** [*Crosses to the fireplace for his glasses.*] I'm doing wrong by Mena, but it can't do any harm if he's only saying goodbye.

**Nanna:** And you won't read it?

**Mike:** [*Suddenly:*] Why … why shouldn't I read it?

**Nanna:** Ah wouldn't you know yourself the little private things they had between them. If the letter was opened she would only throw it in your face and she'd hate you more for it. Leave the letter sealed. It is a kind of a thing a girl would like to have for a keepsake after she'd be married.

**Mike:** [*In a quandary.*] You're very anxious I shouldn't read it.

**Nanna:** Did I read it myself? And I have it before you. You made a promise you'd give it. Stick to your promise.

**Mike:** [*Irritably:*] I'll stick to my promise.

**Nanna:** God will reward you, Mike … [*The dogs bark.*] You're a good son in your heart.

[NANNA *exits quickly to her room.*

MIKE *looks at the letter for a few moments. He places it on the mantelpiece and looks at it for a moment longer. He takes a brush and crosses to sweep around the meal sacks.*

*The door opens and* THOMASHEEN *enters, dressed as usual. He gives his usual furtive glances.*]

**Thomasheen:** There was a great housekeeper lost in you. You have the games and the antics of a woman the way you handle the brush.

Mike: You are in great fettle at the heel of the day!

Thomasheen: What is the news by you?

Mike: News! What news would I have, man, that was in the depth of the bog all day, footin' turf?

Thomasheen: Are they back from town yet?

Mike: [*Innocently:*] And what would anyone be doing in town?

Thomasheen: [*Laughs.*] Oh, wisha Mike, will you not be playing Moll the Wag? Who is in town but herself and the girl. Didn't I see Seán Dóta giving Mena £50 to buy finery for tomorrow's wedding.

Mike: God gave you great eyes.

Thomasheen: He gave them to the right man. £50 was a great bundle of money for a bit of clothes.

Mike: [*Defensively:*] It was given for Sive's clothes and it will be spent on Sive's clothes.

Thomasheen: [*Crossing to the fire:*] Given for Sive but the two of us know that Mena will have £40 out of the £50 for herself.

Mike: You're a great mind for putting and taking with sums of money.

Thomasheen: God gave me that, too. Sure, what harm is it if herself makes a few pounds in the buying of the clothes. Doesn't she deserve it. She worked hard for the wedding, God knows. [*Turns and walks towards the window.*]

[MIKE *does not answer. He crosses to the fire. He glances around to see* THOMASHEEN *looking out of the window and furtively takes the letter to hide in his pocket. As he is doing so,* THOMASHEEN *turns suddenly.*]

Thomasheen: What is that?

**Mike:**       Nothing!

**Thomasheen:**  Since when did Mike Glavin start putting nothing into his pocket?

**Mike:**       Well, if your mind is that curious, it was a letter, although it's none of your business or mine but as little.

**Thomasheen:**  [*Laughs.*] Until I have a hundred sovereigns in my breast pocket, I will make business out of everything. Who is the letter for?

**Mike:**       Sive.

**Thomasheen:**  Sive, is it? And who is it from?

**Mike:**       How would I know? Bocock the tinker handed it in, passing the way. I'm keeping it for her.

**Thomasheen:**  [*Alert and serious. Then, with alarm:*] And the letter is for Sive?

**Mike:**       That's what I told you! Somebody wishing her well, I suppose, on the eve of her wedding.

**Thomasheen:**  And what will you do with the letter?

**Mike:**       I will give it to Sive, of course, when she lands from town. What else would I do with it?

**Thomasheen:**  It comes to me now and again about you!

**Mike:**       What comes to you?

**Thomasheen:**  It comes to me that you are the greatest lump of a fool, of an eejit, of a dul amú, in the seven parishes. You shouldn't be trusted with a quenched match. How do you know what is in the letter? Wishing her well, how are you? If you ever get out of the bog and put a few days aside for journeying there is an asylum for lunatics where you could put down a bit of time without doing yourself any harm.

**Mike:**       [*Frowns, in misunderstanding.*] It is only a letter.

**Thomasheen:**  [*Mimics* MIKE.] Only a letter!

**Mike:** What harm could be in a few words of writing?

**Thomasheen:** [*Patiently:*] Aaah! My dotey God! What would be in it but thoughts to disturb her young head the night before her marriage. Have you no knowledge of the way a woman do be the night before? Turning and twisting and wondering if she is doing right or wrong. A woman never knows from one minute to the next what way her mind is going to act. 'Tis their affliction. 'Tis the way they are made. You must make up the mind for them. You must whip them up and keep them going, or, like a giddy heifer on the road to the fair, the next thing you know she'll let a screech out of her, cock her tail up high in the air and break through the first gap in a hedge into some other man's land, and be content there.

**Mike:** What signifies that?

**Thomasheen:** Little you know! Open the letter and read out the contents of it.

**Mike:** It isn't your letter.

**Thomasheen:** Will you take it out of your pocket and not be playing the gom?

**Mike:** [*Taking out the letter.*] But it is Sive's letter and it is marked 'Private' with a red pencil.

**Thomasheen:** If it was marked with green, white and yellow and sealed with a bishop's ring it will have to be opened. Will you not be tormenting me now, and open it.

**Mike:** [*Yielding.*] But, sure, what harm …?

**Thomasheen:** [*Assumes a tearful tone, in mockery.*] Will you open it or you'll drive me to Gleann na nGealt where your own equals do be.

**Mike:** [*Pause.*] Isn't she getting married tomorrow. Let her have the letter. 'Tis private, look.

[*He holds the letter at arm's length. With a swift adroit movement* THOMASHEEN *snatches the letter and tears it open. He takes the sheets*

78

*of folded notepaper from the envelope and opens them. He looks at them and hands them to* MIKE.]

**Thomasheen:** Read!

**Mike:** Read yourself!

**Thomasheen:** I had no time for schoolin' when I was a boy. Read it now an' don't be makin' trouble for yourself.

[MIKE *takes the letter hesitantly and peruses the first page.*]

**Mike:** [*Disgustedly:*] You read it! That's Sive's letter.

[MIKE *hands the letter back to* THOMASHEEN *who holds up his hand in rejection.*]

**Thomasheen:** [*Embarrassed:*] Will you not be mocking. The letter is only like the print of a bird's claw in snow to me. [*Then, firmly:*] You read it out or I'll take it the road down to Seamus Dónal's.

**Mike:** [*Resignedly:*] All right! All right! I'll read it but it goes against the grain by me.

[MIKE *takes a pair of spectacles from his breast-pocket and commences to read. His voice is slow, laborious, hardly doing justice to the letter.*]

**Mike:** [*Reading:*] 'My dearest Sive ...'

**Thomasheen:** Aaah!

**Mike:** [*Concentrates on letter which presents him with a difficult problem. Reading:*] 'My dearest Sive, you may remember the last time I spoke to you when I met you coming from school ...'

**Thomasheen:** Go on! [*He enjoys himself beyond measure.*] Go on, let you! Do it say there who 'tis from?

**Mike:** [*Finds end of the letter and reads:*] 'Yours eternally, Liam.'

**Thomasheen:** Oh, boys! Oh, boys!

**Mike:** [*Coughs, reads:*] '... I have heard from Carthalawn and Pats Bocock, the tinker-poets, that you are getting married to Seán Dóta, the farmer ...'

**Thomasheen:** Would you say now that it was a private letter?

|               | [*Triumphantly:*] Would you say now that it shouldn't be read? [*Contemptuously:*] Go on, man, and read the contents of it. |
|---------------|---|

**Mike:** '... Sive, my dearest Sive, I find it impossible to believe that you are marrying this wizened little man of your own accord [*reading faster*] ... do you not remember the nights, the starry nights, we spent together in the deep of the bog. There was the quiet and the peace of what we felt for each other. I loved you then, Sive. I love you now ...'

**Thomasheen:** He did, indeed! Aha! the scoundrel! Breaking up honest homes. Has he no love for the law of the land and the voice of the priest?

**Mike:** Will you hold your tongue and let me finish! [*Worried tone:*] 'You are certain to think here that I am beginning to wax poetic ...'

**Thomasheen:** Wax? [*Loudly:*] He's wax from head to heel! [*Knowingly:*] He will never have a woman the way he is going about it! There is no wax in the ketching of women. There is the ketchin' of a hoult until she is winded. That's the time for words with a woman.

**Mike:** Do you want me to read the letter or will I leave it?

**Thomasheen:** Go on! Go on, blast you! You're mad for the word on paper. [MIKE *turns over a page and continues, for a moment master of the situation because he can read, also obviously impressed by the sincerity of the letter.*]

**Mike:** [*Reading:*] '... so I have made a decision with regard to you. I believe you are being forced into this marriage against your will. If that is the case and I hope with all my heart that it is, I beg of you Sive, to do as I say. Tonight when they have all gone to bed, steal away quietly and come to my house. I will be waiting there for you. We will drive straight to the city and be married there the first thing. Remember, I will wait for you through the whole night ...'

**Thomasheen:** Oh, the juice of the roses! Oh, the blood of the grape!

**Mike:** [*Reading:*] '… if you do not come, I will take it that you are content with your choice.'

**Thomasheen:** Oh, the moon and the stars!

**Mike:** 'If this be so, goodbye and God keep you safe. Yours eternally, Liam.'

**Thomasheen:** Ah! They had it well planned! God always finds out a rogue. Trying to steal away the poor innocent girl in the dark of the night.

[MIKE *folds the letter and places it on the table. He takes off his glasses, and lifts the torn envelope from the ground. It is obvious that the letter has rattled him.*]

**Mike:** What will we do?

**Thomasheen:** I don't know! [*As* MIKE *is preoccupied with his thoughts,* THOMASHEEN *takes the letter in the tongs and burns it over the fire.*]

**Mike:** [*Angrily:*] What are you doing?

[MIKE *tries to snatch the letter but* THOMASHEEN *roughly pushes him away. He drops the letter and envelope to the ground.*]

**Thomasheen:** Leave it burn! What she don't know won't trouble her. Our man will have a long wait below. [*He crushes the burning letter under his foot.*]

**Mike:** The letter was Sive's!

**Thomasheen:** Will you hold your tongue, you bleddy oinseach! Keep your gob shut. There's the noise of the pony and car on the bohareen. Forget about the letter. You don't know the harm you might cause. When she comes, pretend nothing.

**Mike:** God direct me, but am I doing right by the girl at all? [*He says this half to himself.*]

**Thomasheen:** In the honour of God will you be one way or the other, will you? … Will you? … [*Raises his voice.*] You're like

81

an oul' hen, dodgin' an dartin', not knowin' what way to turn. Straighten yourself out, man, and be your age for one time in your life.

[THOMASHEEN *goes to the window and looks out.*]

**Thomasheen:** They're in the yard … they've the car loaded with stuff … Aha! Cases of porter! The devil knows what!

[THOMASHEEN *turns to the door and rubs his hands together with great delight.* MENA *enters the kitchen. She carries a large brown-papered parcel under one arm and a smaller parcel under the other.*]

**Mena:** [*Crossly:*] 'Tis a wonder one of ye didn't open the door when ye saw me coming with my hands full.

**Mike:** Where is Sive?

**Mena:** She is coming.

[SIVE *enters and stands self-consciously in her new clothes.*]

**Mike:** There's style.

**Mena:** Go out to the car and bring in the boxes and don't be standing there with your hands hanging.

[*Without a word, both men go out,* MIKE *in the lead.* SIVE *takes off a pair of new high-heeled shoes which she is wearing and rubs her soles fondly, religiously, with her right hand, balancing with her left hand resting on the table. Slowly she takes off coat and hat. She wears a smart blue* frock *underneath. She takes the coat and hat to the room near the hearth.* MENA, *the parcels in her hands, goes after* SIVE *into the room.*

*Immediately* MIKE *and* THOMASHEEN *enter, carrying a crate of stout between them.* MIKE *removes a chair from between the dresser and the door and puts the box in its place. He goes to dresser, finds a bottle-opener and deftly uncaps two bottles, one of which he hands to* THOMASHEEN. *He puts the opener in his pocket.*]

**Mike:** Go mbeirimid beo!

**Thomasheen:** Good luck to us all and bad luck to no one!

[*Both drink heartily from the bottles, lower them, lift them secondly in unison and drain the bottles, which they return to the box. They then hurry out to the yard again.*

SIVE *enters the kitchen wearing a pair of low shoes. She sits on a chair near the fire holding her hands in her lap awkwardly.*

THOMASHEEN *and* MIKE *return with a second crate which they put on top of the first. Both look cautiously at* SIVE *and then at each other.* SIVE *does not look up at them.*

MENA *arrives into the kitchen.*]

**Mena:** Will ye hurry up, for God's sake, and bring in the other boxes.

[*Both men go out again and* MENA *places a hand on* SIVE'*s shoulder.*]

**Mena:** We will have a bit to eat now. There are sausages and rashers and sweet cake to follow.

**Sive:** [*Without looking up.*] I'm not hungry. [*Tired and dispirited:*] I think I'll go to bed instead. My head is on fire.

**Mena:** You haven't put a bit inside of you all day. How do you think you will feel if you don't eat?

**Sive:** I don't feel any desire for food. [*Absently:*] I would like to lie down.

[MIKE *and* THOMASHEEN *enter the kitchen again carrying a large tea chest between them.*]

**Mena:** Put it down there! [*They place it aside.*]

**Mike:** I think I will chance a bottle of stout after that.

**Thomasheen:** It never did harm!

[MENA *looks with disapproval at him when* MIKE *extracts two bottles from the upper crate. He returns and hands one to* THOMASHEEN, *having opened both.*]

**Mena:** [*To* MIKE, *with caution:*] Don't you know what that stuff does to you? We'll be having you puking and choking for the rest of the night like a sick cat.

[THOMASHEEN *and* MIKE *drink from the bottles.*]

**Mike:** 'Tis all right, woman! 'Tis all right!

**Thomasheen:** Is the stomach delicate with you?

**Mike:**    [*To* Sive, *in a kind tone:*] Will you have a drop of lemonade, Sive, or maybe a suppeen of wine to warm you?

**Sive:**    [*Sighs.*] No! I have no mind for it.

**Mena:**    [*Not crossly:*] And what will you have? You're not hungry and you're not thirsty. Is there anything you have a mind for?

**Sive:**    [*Shakes her head:*] No, nothing!

**Mena:**    I don't know what to say to you.

**Sive:**    [*Rises, slowly, wearily.*] I think I'll go to bed now.

**Mena:**    The bed is made and ready for you. Maybe you will feel like something later on.

[Sive *walks slowly to her room.* Mena *watches her hard-eyed. Exit* Sive. Mena *goes to dresser and puts three saucers on the table.*]

**Mena:**    Will you go out and untackle the pony. Do you want the poor animal to die on his feet?

[Mike *finishes his bottle, places it in the crate and hurries out closing the door.* Mena *returns to the dresser and puts out three cups on the saucers.*]

**Thomasheen:** Well?

**Mena:**    Well, what?

**Thomasheen:** Is everything going right with the girl?

**Mena:**    I told you there is no need to worry about that part of it. Mind you collect what is due to us in the morning.

**Thomasheen:** When the ring is on her finger, I'll handle the money. There is no fear Seán Dóta will part with a farthing before his time.

**Mena:**    Oh, you needn't tell me!

**Thomasheen:** He gave you £50 to buy finery. [*He advances with bottle in hand.*]

**Mena:**    It was wanted!

**Thomasheen:** You could buy out a shop for £50.

**Mena:** He gave me the money, me to do what I liked with it. I bought the best, and if there is a shilling or two left over who is better entitled to it than me?

**Thomasheen:** There was a letter from Liam Scuab for Sive!

**Mena:** What!

**Thomasheen:** He was for giving it to her. [*He indicates outside where* MIKE *has gone.*]

**Mena:** The fool! Where is the letter now? Where is it?

**Thomasheen:** Calm yourself, woman! Calm yourself! I took it from him and burned it.

**Mena:** A good night's work!

**Thomasheen:** And what way is the old woman?

**Mena:** I am from the house all day. She never appeared yesterday or the day before.

**Thomasheen:** Just as well.

[*The door opens and* MIKE *enters. Immediately he takes a bottle from the crate.* THOMASHEEN *drains his quickly and puts it in the crate. He takes the bottle from* MIKE's *hand and hands another from the crate to* MIKE.

*Leisurely* MIKE *thrusts his hand into his trousers pocket and produces the opener.* THOMASHEEN *holds the bottle steady whilst* MIKE *uncaps it.* MIKE *uncaps his own and sits on the sacks.*

THOMASHEEN *sits upon the tea chest. Both raise the bottles to their mouths and quaff deeply.*]

**Mena:** Ye will have nothing left the way ye're going. Tomorrow is to come yet, take care.

**Mike:** [*Lifting his bottle to remonstrate:*] Only a few oul' bottles of porter.

**Thomasheen:** [*Who is a joy unto himself.*] We will be in the middle of plenty soon!

**Mike:** There is company, the road up. I saw him far down …

**Mena:** [*Much interested:*] Who is that?

**Mike:** Dóta! [*Lifts bottle and drinks.*]

**Thomasheen:** Long life!

**Mike:** Long life to us!

**Mena:** Seán Dóta?

**Mike:** Seán Dóta, the farmer! [*Drinks.*]

**Mena:** Will you go aisy with that! D'you remember the last time you drank porter. D'you remember the state of the room after you. You're like a pet bonham snugglin' and sucklin' for all the good it's doing you. Will you ever come to the age of sense?

**Thomasheen:** [*Solemnly:*] It might be safer to give no drink to what's comin'! If he had a fall on the road and gave over life wouldn't we be in a nice state with the whole country laughing at us in the morning.

**Mena:** He's in safe-keeping here. [*Raises her head and listens.*] Hold aisy! He's down on the door!

[THOMASHEEN *suddenly comes to his feet and withdraws to the far side of the working-table. Delicately he lifts the bottle to his lips, and drinks slowly, keeping his eye on the door. There is a timid knock on the door.* MENA *goes to it and opens the door.* SEÁN DÓTA *enters, apologetically and with his customary half-laugh he salutes them.*]

**Thomasheen:** Mind your head, Seán.

**Mena:** Seán, will you sit up to the fire?

**Seán Dóta:** [*Who is dressed as before, raises a deprecatory hand and laughs apologetically.*] No fire for me, thank you. No fire. [*He surveys the kitchen, hands behind his back.*]

**Thomasheen:** [*Closing the front door.*] Soon enough you will have the fire to your side, you diggle, you!

**Seán Dóta:** [*Laughs apologetically.*] Ho-ho! the joker! [*He shakes his head.*]

**Mena:** Will you sit down? You must be a bundle of nerves in wait for the morning?

**Seán:**    [*Laughingly:*] Oh, wisha, indeed now! I came to see if all was right.

**Mike:**    Rest yourself Seán! All is right!

[SEÁN *sits on the chair to the right of the kitchen table.*]

**Mena:**    Sive is resting in her room.

**Seán:**    The bit of rest is good.

**Mike:**    The weather is holding up fine.

**Seán:**    The rain is threatening this long time. [*Laughs.*] When 'twill fall 'twill fall heavy, I'm thinking. 'Twill be no harm. Won't it give rise to growth.

**Thomasheen:**  True for you.

[MENA *goes to the dresser and takes out small plates which she distributes about the table. She bends to the lower part and takes out a large plate of home-baked bread. The men keep talking.*]

**Mike:**    There is talk of the milk rising.

**Seán:**    [*Laughs.*] No harm indeed to rise it. Great waste going into the feeding of cows. Ye are celebrating, I see.

**Mike:**    So well we might, it being the night it is!

**Seán:**    [*Laughs.*] Oho!

[MENA *takes knives and spoons from dresser and puts them on table. She slices the bread.*]

**Mike:**    Will you take something yourself, Seán?

**Seán:**    [*Laughs.*] Oho! [*He casts a quick glance at the crate of bottles.*]

**Mike:**    It never poisoned a man yet.

**Seán:**    [*Laughs.*] Well ... I suppose ...

**Mena:**    [*Turns to* SEÁN, *with knife up-raised in her hand.*] No man should taste the taste of drink the night before his marriage.

**Mike:**    That's true.

**Mena:**      I will pour out a nice bottle of lemonade for you, now, Seán.

**Seán:**      Don't mind me! I'll just sit here for myself.

**Mena:**      I'll put a place at the table for you.

[MENA *goes to the dresser and puts out another cup and saucer on the table. She then takes a jug from the dresser and fills it from the tank, drying the bottom of it with a cloth. She puts the jug on the table.*]

**Mike:**      [*Raises a hand for silence.*] Whisht yeerselves!

[*They all listen attentively, then unmistakably comes the sound of a bodhrán in the distance, growing in volume. THOMASHEEN slips unobtrusively to the fire and puts his back to it, fearfully.*]

**Thomasheen:**  'Tis Bocock and his son.

**Mike:**      Come in, let you.

[*The tapping of the stick is heard upon the door, in time with the bodhrán. PATS and CARTHALAWN appear in the doorway. CARTHALAWN is playing and singing.*]

**Carthalawn:**  Come now listen while I sing
To the blessing that I bring
To the bridegroom and his lovely bride so fair
May they dwell in wedded joy
May they ever hear the cry
Of a new big bouncing baby every year.

**Mike:**      Great work! Great work! Ye're welcome to these parts. Will ye drink porter?

[MENA *stands by, arms folded, scowling.*]

**Pats:**      We will indeed! We saw the boxes coming up the tar road with the porter-bottles buck-jumping inside in them. I would follow a box of porter to the gates of hell and beyond it if I was dry.

[MIKE *takes two bottles from the crate, opens them, and hands them to CARTHALAWN and PATS. He replaces his own empty bottle and opens another for himself.*]

**Pats:**      That we might never want!

[PATS *toasts* MIKE, MIKE *quaffs his bottle.* PATS *and* CARTHALAWN *empty their bottles at one swallow.* MIKE *returns to his chair with his bottle.*]

**Mike:**    Let ye sit down?

**Pats:**    We would sooner stand.

**Mike:**    Ye know all here?

**Pats:**    We do, indeed.

**Mike:**    Ye know Seán Dóta, who is for marriage in the morning?

**Pats:**    [*Meaningly:*] We know the farmer.

**Mike:**    What is the news from the country?

**Pats:**    There is money-making everywhere. The face of the country is changing. The small man with the one cow and the pig and the bit of bog is coming into his own. He is pulling himself up out of the mud and the dirt of the years. He is coming away from the dunghill and the smokey corner. The shopkeeper is losing his stiffness. 'Tis only what I see in my travels. The farmer will be the new lord of the land. What way will he rule? What way will he hould up under the new riches? There will be great changes everywhere. The servant boy is wearing the collar and tie. The servant girl is painting and powdering and putting silkified stockings on her feet and wearing frilly small clothes under her dress. 'Tis only what I see in my travels. The servant will kick off the traces and take to the high road. Money will be in a-plenty. [*He points at* SEÁN DÓTA.] The likes of him will be the new lords of the land. God help the land!

**Mena:**    You're full of dare to insult a dacent respectable man in my house.

**Pats:**    'Tis only what I see in my travels, a-woman – only what I see in my travels.

89

**Thomasheen:** Well, ye can be travelling out of here now. The cheek of ye!

**Pats:** Carthalawn! Your best! [*He taps with his stick.*] Your mighty best!

[PATS *taps with his stick again and* CARTHALAWN *takes up the time. Then the sounds decrease and* CARTHALAWN *sings.*]

**Carthalawn:**　May he screech with awful thirst
　　　　　　　May his brains and eyeballs burst
　　　　　　　That melted amadawn, that big bostoon,
　　　　　　　May the fleas consume his bed
　　　　　　　And the mange eat up his head,
　　　　　　　That black man from the mountain, Seánín Rua.

**Mike:** Great work! Great work! [*He slaps his knee with his hand in glee.*]

**Seán:** Ho-ho! Ho-ho!

[THOMASHEEN *fumes with rage.* MENA *scowls at the tinkers.*]

**Mike:** Ye never lost it! 'Pon my word, ye never lost it!

**Seán:** [SEÁN DÓTA *rises.*] I will be for the road. God knows, I will have an early start in the morning.

**Mena:** Will you wait till I call Sive up from the room. She will be dying to see you before you go.

**Seán:** [*Changes his mind quickly and sits on the chair again.*] By God! I'll wait a minute or two, so!

[MENA *goes into the room by the hearth.* PATS *sweeps off his hat and holds it in front of* SEÁN.]

**Pats:** Something to bring luck to you! A handful of silver!

**Seán:** How soft you have it! Money for nothing, how are you?

[PATS *retreats dignified to stand in line with his son.*]

**Mike:** You must be getting tired, Seán? I know what is the feeling of a day before marriage.

**Pats:** It will be a rest for the poor man to marry.

**Seán:** [*Laughs.*] A rest?

**Pats:** The young girl will be the death of you.

**Seán:** How dare you! How dare you, tinker?

**Pats:** A squeeze out of a lively young girl would stop your heart, old man. Cathalawn, your best! Your mighty best!

**Carthalawn:** [*Sings:*] May his hens lay clods and stones
May the east wind blight his bones
May warts and welts waylay him by the score.
Now I swear upon this verse
He'll be travelling soon by hearse
And we'll never see Seán Dóta anymore.

**Mena:** [*Re-entering, hysterically.*] She's gone! There's a bundle of clothes under the quilt where she should be lying. She's after stealing away on us!

**Thomasheen:** [*Seizes her by the arm, roughly.*] What are you screeching about? Catch a hould of yourself.

**Mena:** She's gone, I tell you! The window of the room is open!

**Thomasheen:** Did she take baggage with her?

**Mena:** No! ... No! ... Nothing! not even a shoe for her feet.

**Thomasheen:** Would she have stolen around to the old woman's room?

[MENA *breaks from his grasp and hurries to* NANNA'*s room to look in.*]

**Thomasheen:** [*Loudly:*] Well? Is she there?

**Mike:** [*Stands up.*] Where could she have gone at this hour of the night, without a shoe or a coat on her?

**Pats:** There was something a while ago and we coming up from the cross.

**Thomasheen:** Out with it! What?

**Pats:** [*Frowning.*] It may be that my eyes would be fooling me but I thought I saw the figure of a girl flashing across the bog near the end of the cutaway where the deep holes do be. I thought it might be a shadow.

**Mena:** [*Composed again:*] And why didn't you say so when you came?

**Pats:** How was I to know if the sight of my eyes was going or coming? It was only now that you talk about the girl that I think it might have been the girl, Sive.

**Thomasheen:** You oul' bocock! you oul' dirty twisted bocock! Damn well you knew!

**Pats:** I did not know, and what is it to me if all the people of the parish ran over the bog in the middle of the night with bare feet.

**Mena:** What if she fell into a hole ... Oh, my God! [*She shrieks at* MIKE.] Find her! Find her! ... Hurry yourself!

**Mike:** I'll get a lantern in the stable ...

[MENA *rushes to the room by the fireplace and returns almost immediately with the rubber waders.* MIKE *kicks off his shoes and pulls on the waders.*]

**Thomasheen:** I will go with you.

**Seán Dóta:** I will go along with ye.

**Mena:** Stay, Seán! I will not stay here alone by myself. Stay, somebody. Stay with me. I won't be alone!

[*From outside, a frantic voice is heard.*]

**Liam:** Show light! ... Show light! ... Leave open the door ... I am coming over the bog.

[THOMASHEEN *opens the door fully.* MENA *hurries with the oil lamp to the door.* MIKE *hurries to the door. All exchange frightened glances.*

*They retreat from the door as* LIAM *draws near. Their faces are horrified as they stand back.*

*Enter* LIAM. *He is bareheaded and his clothes are wet. His face is ghastly pale. In his arms he carries* SIVE. *Her hair is plastered to her head and her slight body hangs limp in* LIAM's *arms.* LIAM *advances without looking to left or right. At the table he stops.*

PATS *comes forward and with his stick sweeps the table clean. The ware clatters on the ground breaking the silence. Reverently* LIAM *lays the motionless body on the table.*

*The water drips on to the floor from both* LIAM *and* SIVE. LIAM *folds* SIVE's *hands across her breast.* MENA *replaces the lamp.*]

**Liam:**        A cloth to dry her hair!

[MENA *hands* LIAM *a cloth.* THOMASHEEN *edges in to look at the body, then horrified, edges slyly away and exits, looking around him furtively. He is noticed only by* SEÁN DÓTA *who follows him, backing, sneaking, to the door.* SEÁN *exits.*]

**Liam:**        [*Tearfully:*] I saw her running across the bog with only the little frock against the cold of the night. She ran like the wind and she letting cries out of her that would rend your heart. [*Filled with sorrow:*] I called after her but she would not stop. She took her own life. It was a while before I found her. The poor tormented child.

**Mena:**        Drowned, dead.

[LIAM *turns suddenly on* MENA, *blazing with anger.*]

**Liam:**        [*Cries in anguish:*] You killed her! You ... you ... you killed her! You horrible filthy bitch! That the hand of Jesus may strike you dead where you stand. You heartless wretch that hunted the poor little girl to her grave.

[MENA *retreats, shocked, before him, her hand stupidly covering her mouth.*]

**Liam:**        [*Shrieks:*] Go away! ... Go away! ... You are polluting the pure spirit of the child with your nearness. Go away, witch!

[LIAM *raises the towel clenched in his fist to strike* MENA. MENA *hurries away back to her room,* LIAM *begins to dry* SIVE's *hair with the cloth, lovingly and with care.*]

**Liam:**     The beautiful hair of her! [*He takes her hand.*] The
          lovely silky white of her!

**Mike:**     [*Stupidly, idiotically:*] The priest ... we must go for the
          priest ... she must have the priest ... Holy ground ...
          she must be buried in holy ground ... the priest ... I
          must go for the priest ...

[LIAM *gives* MIKE *a scalding look.*]

**Liam:**     Go for the priest then! ... Go on! ... Go!

[MIKE *seizes* LIAM *by the two hands.*]

**Mike:**     I can't go alone! ... There's no luck in going for a
          priest alone. You know the old saying ...

[MIKE *is foolish, babbling now.* LIAM *shakes off* MIKE's *hands violently.*
*He seizes* MIKE *by the hand and drags him to the door.*]

**Liam:**     Come on! ... I'll lead you past where she was drowned.
          You'll be on the tar road then. You'll find company.

[*They both go out leaving* PATS *and* CARTHALAWN *alone with* SIVE.
*After a moment* CARTHALAWN *goes forward and touches* SIVE's *face
with his hand. His face is sad as he looks at her. After a few seconds* PATS
*taps with his stick and* CARTHALAWN *draws away slowly. Both men
stand to attention. Then, gently, the stick taps, the knuckles very gently
tap the bodhrán to slow time. Slow of voice and tenderly* CARTHALAWN
*sings.* PATS *looks at him tenderly.*]

**Carthalawn:**  [*Singing:*] Oh, come all good men and true,
              A sad tale I'll tell to you
              All of a maiden fair, who died this day;
              Oh, they drowned lovely Sive,
              She would not be a bride
              And they laid her for to bury in the clay.

[*They turn slowly and march slowly in step through the door,*
CARTHALAWN *still singing gently.*]

**Carthalawn:**  Oh, come all good men and true
              A sad tale I'll tell to you
              All of a maiden fair, who died this day.

Oh, they murdered lovely Sive,
She would not be a bride,
And they laid her dead, to bury in the clay.

[*The singing fades, slowly, slowly, as the light fades in the kitchen.*

NANNA, *in the faint light comes slowly from her room and goes to where* SIVE *is lying. She bows her head over the dead body and weeps silently.*

*The singing fades away altogether.*]


## FINAL CURTAIN

# CHARACTERS

## NANNA GLAVIN

While Nanna Glavin has admirable integrity in crucial moments of the play, she is by no means an angelic, mild character. Although Mena is hateful and abusive to her, Nanna has the fiery spirit and temper to give as good as she gets. She detests Mena and is discontent to be replaced as female head of the house: 'I was here before you'. It was custom at the time that the older woman would acknowledge the incoming daughter-in-law as chief organiser of the home and farm, but Nanna does not wish to relinquish her status too readily: 'Am I to be scolded night and day in my own house?'

She can be provocative and hurtful to Mena, particularly in her repetitive, hard-hitting comments about her childlessness: 'ah, you'd burn well, for you're as dry as the hobs of hell inside of you. Every woman of your age in the parish has a child of her own and nothing to show by you'. She also makes cutting comments on Mena's poverty-stricken background: 'Your father, a half-starved bocock of a beggar'. She also does not hesitate to castigate Mena behind her back to Mike: 'I mean that pauperised wretch you call a wife'.

For all her faults, audiences invariably empathise with Nanna's harsh situation. Her testy relationship with the volatile, uncompromising Mena must be a terrible burden to bear. Nanna adores Sive. She is devastated at the match and is not afraid to voice her disapproval: 'There is a hatchery of sin in this house'. She is Sive's closest confidante and knows about her secret sweetheart, Liam Scuab. We really feel sorry for Nanna when Mena and Thomasheen Seán Rua launch a vicious, menacing attack on her: 'Go on! Put your bag on your back and go begging from door to door'.

In spite of being threatened with being sent to the dreaded county home where she will not be permitted to smoke her pipe, Nanna does her utmost to prevent Sive's marriage to Seán Dóta. She pleads passionately with her son, Mike to put a stop to the proposed marriage: 'How can I go aisy when my own grand-child is for sale like an animal?' She defends Liam Scuab's character to Mike asserting that he is a 'gradhbhar boy' who is genuine and trustworthy: 'there's a sweet thing to their love'. She even conspires with Pats Bocock to deliver a letter to Sive which would allow her to elope with Scuab. She is perhaps foolish, naïve and imprudent when she trusts Mike with the letter – who unwittingly hands it over to Thomasheen Seán Rua.

Nanna's absolute heart-break at Sive's death is sensitively and poignantly expressed when Keane places her at the very end of the play. Audiences cannot but be moved when she emerges from her room to pay her own private farewell to her beloved grand-daughter.

## MENA GLAVIN

Mena Glavin is one of the most formidable female presences to grace an Irish stage. She is dissatisfied with her life, bitterly lamenting the miserable match she made with Mike Glavin: 'Look at the match I made – four cows on the top of the mountain and a few acres of bog'. She is a hard worker and claims to have built up the farm single-handedly with her endeavours.

Mena has a troubled, tense relationship with her mother-in-law, Nanna Glavin. There is fierce animosity between them. Nanna despises Mena and takes every opportunity to insult her family background and to chide her for her childlessness. Meanwhile, an angry Mena responds vitriolically and hatefully to Nanna's scathing comments constantly scolding her for smoking her pipe: 'Some day that pipe will take fire where you have it hidden and you'll go off in a big, black ball of smoke and ashes'.

Mena is bad-tempered, curt and cantankerous throughout the play. She seems jealous of the close bond between Nanna and Sive. She treats Sive with disdain and begrudges rearing her and paying for her education. Thomasheen Seán Rua knows that Mena has the cunning and calculating reserves to consent to something as outrageous as a match with Seán Dóta. He purposefully seeks her out as he knows she has the metal and ambition to see the match through: 'I knew my woman from the start'. A merciless Mena sees the match as a chance for her to be rid of Nanna and to acquire the coveted £200.

Indeed, money is of huge significance to Mena: 'How much for the single bonham?' She is thrifty and abhors waste, reprimanding Nanna and Sive for wasting oil with the lamp. She is mean and miserly when she refuses Pats Bocock tea and sugar. However, her care in the management of money may be a sign of the terrible hard times farmers had to endure: 'we will mind whatever penny we have'.

Mena slowly and skilfully connives to convince Mike Glavin to agree to the match. She cleverly uses Mike's love for money to her advantage: 'There is the gift of 200 pounds for us …' She avails of every trick and tactic at her disposal to bring him round to her way of thinking. She mocks his manhood: 'Go away! Go away with you. Go away, man of straw'. Mena uses her sexuality to charm and coax him, thanks to the advice of her mentor, Thomasheen Seán Rua: 'Aren't ye in the one bed sleeping?'

Mena will do and say anything to get what she wants. She cruelly upsets and overwhelms a vulnerable Sive with the history of her birth: 'You have no name. You will have no name till you take a husband'. She knows that by playing on Sive's insecurities, she will crumble and submit to the match, which she inevitably does. To copper-fasten the smooth running of her plans, Mena takes severe measures against Sive. She alienates Sive from Nanna by not allowing them to sleep together. She puts a sudden end to Sive's education, violently flinging Sive's schoolbag across the room. She curtails Sive's movements completely to prevent her from meeting Liam Scuab.

Mena will stop at nothing to attain her goals. She vindictively intimidates and bullies Nanna, with Thomasheen Seán Rua, threatening destitution: 'She's enough of a burden without becoming a curse altogether'. She physically threatens Liam Scuab: 'I'll open you! I'll open you if you vex me more'. She is perhaps at her most frightful when she lies to Sive claiming that Liam Scuab called just to wish her the best on her wedding day.

Mena is the recipient of a lot of negative criticism in the play. Nanna calls her 'a hungry sow' and 'a greasy bitch'. Liam Scuab accuses her of murdering Sive: 'You heartless wretch that hunted the poor girl to her grave'.

In her defence, Mena is not the classic, conventional villain of melodrama. Emer O'Kelly has stated: 'This was Mena, the woman incapable of softness and love because both had been ground out of her by Ireland, its people, its greed, and its frustrations'. Mena reminds Sive that her own childhood was impoverished and difficult: 'There was no corner of the bed we could call our own'. Her life is a constant struggle trying to make ends meet and her childlessness must be a source of anxiety and agony, especially with the taunts of her adversarial mother-in-law. In her own way, Mena, who sees love and marriage in pragmatic terms, believes she is doing Sive a favour by encouraging her to marry this wealthy farmer: 'Will you thank God that you won't be for the rest of your days working for the bare bite and sup like the poor women of these parts'.

## MIKE GLAVIN

The stage directions inform us that Mike Glavin is 'a quiet man, determined of movement'. Glavin works hard on his farm with his wife, Mena. Money is important to Mike Glavin: 'Money is the best friend a man ever had'. Mena knows that the allure of a substantial dowry for Sive could persuade Mike to acquiesce to the match. Mena remarks to Thomasheen Seán Rua: 'He has a great love for the few pounds'.

Mike Glavin is initially completely against the match, seeing himself as the father Sive never had: 'She has no father. I have responsibility'. He is determined and insistent that the match should not go ahead: 'Never ... if the sun, moon and stars rained down out of the heavens and split the ground under my feet ... never'. Yet the fear of the past repeating itself, with Liam Scuab romantically linked to Sive, dramatically alters his view of the match. He is suspicious of Liam Scuab, as Liam is related to Sive's father who Mike believes wronged his sister. Glavin is evidently emotionally scarred by his sister's death and takes out his distress on Liam Scuab: 'You'd better be going, Scuab, or I'll take the whip to you'.

Mike Glavin is weak and ineffectual when faced with the persuasive, domineering Mena. Mena taunts him, suggesting he is meek and unmanly in not approving the match. Eventually the knowledge that Sive has had secret meetings with Liam Scuab breaks Mike Glavin down and forces him to accept the match.

Mike Glavin is a sensitive character and utters some of the most poignant and poetical lines of the play: 'It would be like tossing the white flower of the canavaun on to the manure heap'. He genuinely adores Sive. 'You were better than a father to her', Nanna remarks to him. As the play continues, Mike Glavin reveals serious reservations about the match. He realises that Sive is very unhappy and he begins to have second thoughts about his decision: 'She has no heart for it'. However, he does not act on these doubts and allows himself be over-ruled by Mena's tyranny. Again, his soft, compassionate side is portrayed when he consents to giving Sive the letter from Liam Scuab. He is naïve and credulous in assuming that the contents of the letter are harmless, so much so that Thomasheen Seán Rua upbraids him for being so gullible: 'It comes to me that you are the greatest lump of a fool, of a dul amú in seven parishes'.

Mike Glavin is tormented by the antagonistic relationship between his mother and wife. He is torn between these two strong women: 'It's hard to be a good son and a good husband under the same roof'. The strain of living in such a stormy environment must be intolerable: 'Am I to have no rest from ye?'

As the wedding day approaches, Glavin's conscience troubles him even more and he becomes increasingly agitated: 'God direct me but am I doing right by the girl at all'. On the night before the wedding he drinks at a furious pace to suppress his disquiet. The death of Sive will undoubtedly take a terrible toll on Mike Glavin.

## SEÁN DÓTA

Seán Dóta is not a fully developed character as such. The stage directions reveal that he is aged between 55 and 70 and that he is 'a small man, a little wizened'. He is a prosperous farmer in the community with 'the grass of twenty cows' and 'a servant boy' and 'a servant girl' in his employment. According to Thomasheen Seán Rua, he has been searching for a woman for years: 'How many years have he spent searching the country for a woman?'

He is clearly an undesirable and unsuitable match for Sive. He is physically obsessed with her and purposefully engages the services of the matchmaker, Thomasheen Seán Rua so that he can marry her. 'He will have anything, I tell you, if he will get Sive', Thomasheen confides in Mena. When Mena slyly contrives for Seán Dóta to accompany Sive to a neighbour's house on a so-called errand, he terrifies and repulses Sive by making a pass at her: 'When we passed by the cumar near Dónal's he made a drive at me! He nearly tore the coat off me!' Pats Bocock knows that Dóta's attraction for Sive is solely fuelled by desire and lust: 'He have no love for her. 'Tis the flesh of her he do be doting over'. Liam Scuab also tells the Glavins that he overheard Dóta making crude, unsavoury comments about Sive, 'not fit to mention' as he walked the road.

Seán Dóta initially comes across as a foolish, shallow old man, particularly when he recites some nonsensical, childlike verses in Glavins' house: 'Seánín Easter di-do-dom/Stole a pratey from his mom'. In actuality, he is quite shrewd and self-serving: 'There is no fear Seán Dóta will part with a farthing before his time'. He is ungenerous and hot-headed when he dismisses Pats Bocock by refusing to give him money: 'How soft you have it, money for nothing, how are you?' He hastily sneaks away from the Glavin house when Sive is drowned. This suggests his culpability in initiating the match.

Seán Dóta is the antithesis of everything Liam Scuab is and it is easy to understand why Sive would find him off-putting: 'I have nothing against the poets, mind you, but they are filled with roguery and they have the bad tongue on top of it, the thieves'.

## THE TINKERS

The powerful and memorable presence of Pats Bocock and his son Carthalawn invest the play with colour and character. According to Nanna, they are 'the people of the road – travelling people' and are 'above the class beggar'. Pats Bocock has one foot shorter than the other and is scurrilously mocked by Thomasheen Seán Rua for this: 'Will you look at the appearance of them! A short leg and a half-fool'. This father and son duo dress outlandishly and gaudily, breathing life into the bleak backdrop of the Glavin kitchen.

They reside in a caravan and move from place to place, like travelling minstrels, calling to remote rural areas performing for the people of the house and looking for money or food in return. As was the custom, they generously praise the man of the house, Mike Glavin, when they enter the Glavin home first: 'Oh! Mike Glavin, you're the man/you was always in the van/ with a dacent house to old man and gorsoon'. When Mena curtly asks them what they want, Pats Bocock politely requests 'no more than a dorn of sugar and a dusteen of tay'.

Nanna maintains it is unlucky to refuse a man of the road, but Mena does not agree with this philosophy and rudely spurns them, physically barring Nanna from giving them tea and sugar. Mena is unashamedly abusive of Pats Bocock and Carthalawn: 'The cheek of the two biggest robbers walking the roads of Ireland'. Likewise, Thomasheen Seán Rua is openly obnoxious to them criticising them for begging rather than working: 'Go on away to yeer smelly caravan and not be disgustin' respectable people'. Pats Bocock retaliates in a lively fashion to these taunts forcefully tapping his blackthorn stick on the ground instructing Carthalawn to respond vigorously: 'Your best! Your mighty best'. In song, Carthalawn lambasts Thomasheen Seán Rua with vivid, stirring lyrics to the tuneful beat of the bodhrán: 'He's as greedy as a sow/And the crow behind the plough/That black man from the mountain, Seánín Rua'. Indeed, throughout the play, the tinkers show nothing but antipathy for the matchmaker cursing him with flourish: 'May his brains and eyeballs burst/That melted amadawn, that big bostoon'.

Pats Bocock and Carthalawn embody truth, sincerity and moral decency in the play. In a heroic gesture, they help Liam Scuab to devise a plan to rescue Sive from the lecherous Seán Dóta. Pats Bocock knows that Scuab is genuinely in love with Sive: 'The young man have a true heart for her'. Liam Scuab praises them calling them 'the tinker poets' while Seán Dóta viciously rebuffs them when

Pats Bocock asks him for some silver: 'How soft you have it! Money for nothing, how are you?'

The tinkers act like a Greek chorus commenting on the disturbing train of events surrounding the match: 'Oh! They murdered lovely Sive/She would not be a bride/And they laid her for to bury in the clay'.

In rural areas, these men of the road had an important function as bringers of news to people living in isolated places. Pats Bocock provides the Glavin household with an informed and intelligent social commentary on the changing times on the night before the wedding: 'The farmer will be the new lord of the land … There will be great changes everywhere'.

## LIAM SCUAB

Liam Scuab is a carpenter aged about nineteen and is a cousin of Sive's late father. The stage directions inform us that Scuab is 'good-looking and manly, his voice cultured and refined'. Scuab is presented as a gentle, educated and articulate young man who is besotted with Sive. Thomasheen Seán Rua complains about Scuab's use of 'fine words' to woo Sive while Mike Glavin is deeply suspicious of his 'quick words and book-reading'.

Liam Scuab represents the new emerging face of a changing Ireland. He cannot understand the concept of matchmaking: 'Imagine making a marriage between two people who never saw each other before'. He is devoted to Sive and initially he is polite and courteous with the Glavins when he makes representations against the match. He is horrified at the match which he describes as a 'terrible auction'. He goes so far as to promise the Glavins that he will leave the area until Sive is older so as to prevent the match: He has Sive's best interests at heart and cannot bear to have her fall victim to 'that rotting old man with his gloating eyes and trembling hands!' He uses emotive language and striking religious imagery to try to reawaken the Glavins' consciences: 'Will ye stand and watch each other draw the hard, crooked thorns deep into His helpless body?'

Pats Bocock and Nanna believe that Liam Scuab is honourable

and decent in his love for Sive. Liam Scuab is relentless in his pursuit of Sive and does all he can to be with her, trying to elope with her aided by Nanna and Pats Bocock.

When Liam Scuab enters with the corpse of Sive at the close of the play, audiences are struck by the depth of his love for her: 'The beautiful hair of her! The lovely, silky white of her'. He is furious that she had to suffer such anguish. In his hysteria and grief, an enraged Scuab points the finger of blame at Mena for Sive's death: 'You … you … you killed her. You horrible, filthy bitch! That the hand of Jesus may strike you dead where you stand'. Scuab symbolises honesty, justice and compassion in the play.

# SIVE

Sive is 'aged about 18' and attends the local convent secondary school in the nearby town. She is an orphan and lives with her Uncle Mike, Aunt Mena and Nanna Glavin. She is very attached to Nanna Glavin and Mena deeply resents the close bond between them. Mena is cold and hostile towards Sive and does not believe she should be in school: 'Out working with a farmer you should be, my girl, instead of getting your head filled with notions'.

Sive is involved in a secret romance with Liam Scuab and steals out at night to meet him in the privacy of the bog. According to Nanna, 'There is a sweet thing to their love'. Sive is appalled at the tradition of matchmaking: 'It is horrible, Liam. Would you marry somebody you never saw before?'

Sive is a bright, inquisitive and naïve schoolgirl and asks her grandmother many questions about her late parents and the circum-stances surrounding her birth: 'Why wasn't he here by my mother's side when I was born?' She shows perception and insight when she sees through the underhand scheming of Thomasheen Seán Rua and Mena when Mena sends her on an errand with Seán Dóta: 'You know, I think, Gran, it was a plan by them … but it's so hard to believe'. Sive is distressed and bewildered when Seán Dóta makes a pass at her.

Mena plays on Sive's curiosity about her past when she cruelly and callously informs her that she is illegitimate: 'You are a bye-child, common bye-child, a bastard!' Sive is sickened at the prospect of marriage to Seán Dóta and protests her fears to Mena: 'I could never live with that old man. Fancy the thought of waking in the light of day and looking at him with the small head on him'. Mena succeeds in crushing Sive's spirit when she deliberately alienates Sive from her protector and confidante, Nanna, by placing them in separate rooms. She also puts an abrupt end to Sive's education. A defeated, docile Sive submits dutifully to Mena's tyranny. Mena also ensures Sive cannot meet with Liam Scuab by making a virtual prisoner of her in the house.

As the plot intensifies, Sive changes from being lively and vivacious to becoming listless and despondent. When Mena lies to Sive telling her that Liam Scuab called to wish her well on her wedding, Sive is utterly devastated. On the eve of the marriage to Seán Dóta, Sive is very downcast and withdrawn: 'I don't feel any desire for food'. She complains of a headache and wearily retires to her room: 'I think I'll go to bed … my head is on fire'.

At the end of the play when Liam Scuab recovers the corpse of Sive, he discloses that he had earlier seen her running wildly in the bog in a confused, overwrought state: 'She ran like the wind and she letting cries out of her that would rend your heart'. The match with Seán Dóta was the last straw for Sive compelling her to take her own life by drowning in a bog-hole.

The untimely death of Sive has a shocking impact on all of the characters. This 'flower of the parish' symbolises innocence, beauty and virtue in the play. Liam Scuab even goes so far as to suggest that Sive is a Christ-like figure offered up for crucifixion: 'are you forgetting Him who died on Calvary and will ye stand and watch each other draw the hard, crooked thorns deep into His helpless body?'

## THOMASHEEN SEÁN RUA

Thomasheen Seán Rua, the matchmaker, is a colourful, dynamic force in the play. In his forties, the stage directions indicate that 'he is shifty-looking, forever on his guard'. He visits the Glavin household on behalf of the ageing Seán Dóta to make a match for Sive. He intentionally and craftily seeks out Mena to aid and abet him in his machinations. Nanna shows nothing but contempt for him: 'the mean snap is in you and all that went before you'.

While he is uneducated and illiterate, Thomasheen Seán Rua is a master of human manipulation. He artfully and speedily succeeds in getting Mena on his side by promising the Glavins £200 and the guarantee that Nanna would go and live with Sive as part of the match. He cleverly and cunningly coaches Mena on how to coax Sive into agreeing to the match: 'Be silky then, be canny! Take her gentle'. He persuades Mena to use her sexual charms to cajole Mike into approving the match: 'Sleeping or waking you have your husband in the flesh and bone and there is the one will between ye. You will see that he is of the same word as yourself'. He also ensures Mike Glavin's support by convincing him that Liam Scuab is serious about Sive: 'You'll have him coming into the house proposin' next'.

Thomasheen Seán Rua is amoral and unscrupulous. He is remorseless and is completely motivated by money: 'there will be £100 for me'. He is Machiavellian in his approach to the match. He shows no respect for Nanna and subdues her with Mena when she speaks out against the ill-treatment of Sive: 'Sure the county home is filled to the jaws with the likes of her ... walking the road she should be like the rest of her equals'. He ruthlessly pushes Mena to put an end to Sive's freedom to stop her relationship with Liam Scuab: 'We must cut out every chance of their meeting'.

Keane employs demonic imagery to portray the matchmaker's devious, dark side. Nanna remarks to Pats Bocock: 'You are as well off, Pats, without the paw of the devil burning your palm'. In song, Carthalawn curses Thomasheen Seán Rua in vibrant invective: 'May the devil sweep the hairy creature soon'. Pats Bocock avails of vivid animal imagery to convey how reprehensible he can be: 'You are the bladder of a pig, the snout of a sow, you are the leavings of a hound, the sting of a wasp'. When Liam Scuab carries the corpse of Sive into the Glavin kitchen, Thomasheen Seán Rua 'edges in to look at the body then horrified, edges slyly away and exits looking around him furtively'. This stealthy behaviour suggests he realises his own guilt.

For all his shortcomings, Thomasheen Seán Rua does earn our sympathy. He is very cynical about love: 'What do the likes of us know about love?' He blames his father's suicide for ruining his chances of finding love, as the money he had put aside for a marriage to a girl he had a 'wish for' had to go towards his father's funeral. When Thomasheen Seán Rua speaks movingly about how his father's death affected his life, Fintan O'Toole asserts that he changes from being 'a recognisable sociable baddie into being a genuinely tragic figure'. He is another victim of the dire poverty of the times. He is more than likely psychologically damaged from his excruciating past.

We also see his human side as he grumbles about the agony of loneliness: 'I know what it is to be alone in a house when the only word you will hear is a sigh, the sigh of the fire in the hearth dying, with no words to warm you'. All of these traumatic experiences have embittered him and have desensitised his conscience. He also loses heavily at the end of the play as he will not have the promised £100 from Seán Dóta to secure his own marriage to a widow woman in the village.

# CULTURAL CONTEXT/SETTING

'The society he reflected in his world has now vanished'

JOHN A. MURPHY

The stage directions advise us that 'the action of the play takes place in the kitchen of Glavin's small farmhouse in a remote, mountainy part of southern Ireland'. *Sive* is set 'in the recent past, a late evening of a bitter March day'. Since Keane wrote the play in 1959, *Sive* was, in all probability, set in the middle to late 1950s.

## POVERTY

The middle of the twentieth century was a period of exceptional hardship and deprivation in Ireland owing to the lingering after-effects of the Economic War and the severe global downturn in the wake of the Second World War. The country was brought to its knees by mass emigration. Sive's own late father, an emigrant, was killed while coal-mining in England, eighteen years earlier.

Grinding poverty was extensive and it is a harrowing and in-escapable fact of life in the play. There was little to no state aid for the less well-off. The tinkers are poor and resort to begging: 'A decent man gave us the side of a loaf'. Mike and Mena Glavin live simply and frugally. Their lives are filled with anxiety about money. The house is run on a strict budget: 'We will mind whatever money we make'. Neither Mike nor Mena tolerate waste: 'Tea is scarce enough without wasting it this hour of the night'. It must be challenging to try and fund Sive's education and eke out a meagre living on inferior land: 'Look at the match I made – four cows on the top of a mountain and a few acres of bog'. Accordingly, it is easy to understand how, living under such straitened circumstances, the Glavins could become attracted to the chance of a substantial dowry for Sive. 'There is the gift of £200 for us … Long enough we were scraping', Mena tells Mike.

Scarcity of money influences and affects the lives of many of the play's characters. Mena reminisces sorrowfully on her disadvantaged childhood and Thomasheen Seán Rua complains: 'There was a frightful curam of us in my father's house with nothing but a sciath of spuds on the floor to fill us'. The matchmaker admits to Mena that he couldn't afford to wed as he had to pay for his father's funeral with the two pigs he had fattened for marriage. However, Keane hints that there is a glimmer of hope for the economy and by extension for those who work the land. Mike Glavin, at the start of the play, returns home pleased with his takings from the day at the fair and boasts to Mena that the shop-keepers now bow down to him whereas before 'they wouldn't give a half-sack of flour without money down'. At the end of the play, Pats Bocock gives an insightful account of how the farmer has come out of the doldrums: 'The small man with the one cow and the pig and the bit of bog is coming into his own'.

## RELIGION

Keane does not overtly condemn the Catholic Church in the play but rather subtly brings to light the dominant, controlling influence this powerful bastion brought to bear on Irish life at the time. According to historian, John A. Murphy, Keane 'publicly challenged repressive, sexual puritanism and clerical tyrannies'. The church's interference in matters of sexuality is perceptible in the shame and disgrace attached to Sive since she was born out of wedlock without a father: 'the child is born in want of wedlock. That much is well known from one end of the parish to the other. What is before her when she can put no name on her father? ... Who will take her with the slur and the doubt hanging over her?' Mena tries to convince Sive that she will have no identity or respectability until 'you take a husband'.

The repressive authoritarian nature of the Catholic Church is also implied in Mike's terrified reaction to Sive's suicide. Before the 1960s the Church denounced suicide and dictated that anyone who died by suicide should not be permitted to be buried on consecrated ground. Perhaps, to avoid the stern disapproval of the clergy and the awful stigma attached to suicide, Mike insists emphatically that Sive should be buried on holy ground: 'The priest … we must go for the priest … Holy ground … she must be buried in holy ground … the priest … I must go for the priest'.

Religion is of paramount importance in the play to the characters. The play is infused with religions expressions and images as was part and parcel of the natural vernacular of the people: 'saints preserve us', 'God help us', 'your mother the Lord have mercy on her', 'in the honour of God', etc. The respect and deference given to the local priest is shown when Mike shaves himself before he visits the priest to organise the wedding.

While the characters seem to be deeply religious and guided largely by the principles and rigid ethos of the Church, the play also makes mention of curses, the supernatural, superstitions and the devil. These references probably emanate from a pagan pre-Christian Ireland. Thomasheen Seán Rua speaks of the 'phuca' and 'the mad red eyes of him like coals of fire lighting in his head'. The play abounds in lively, potent curses which would have been alien to conventional Church teaching: 'May his hens lay clods and stones/ May the east wind blight his bones'.

## THE ROLE OF THE SEXES

1950s Ireland was, on the whole, male-orientated. The patriarchal nature of society is exemplified in the arrangement of made marriages. Mena made a match with Mike Glavin of her own volition. Matches were not very common in the 1950s and this is why many of the leading characters object so vociferously to Sive's preposterous match with Seán Dóta. However, Sive has no say in her destiny and is brow-beaten into consenting to the match.

Second level education seems to have been a privilege rather than a right for teenage girls at the time. Mena takes umbrage at Sive receiving an education: 'Why should that young rip be sent to a convent every day instead of being out working with a farmer?'

Even though the world of the play is controlled by men, the women of the play are strong, capable and determined. Mena is not the stereotypical, demure, submissive 1950s wife. She works as hard as any man on the farm and is a feisty, ambitious woman who gets the upper hand of her quiet husband through ingenuity and determination. She is aggressive, forceful and dangerous: 'I'll put streaks on you worse than a raddle-stick'. Moreover, Nanna Glavin breaks the mould of the mild, gentle grandmother. She is tough and defiantly strikes out against the exploitation of Sive: 'There is a curse of evil in this house. Your dead sister and my dead daughter will curse it from her grave'.

## CLASS STRUCTURES

Most of the characters in the play seem to be on an equal economic and social footing, in that everyone seems to be overwhelmed by the pervasive poverty. Seán Dóta, the strong farmer, is the only person of means: 'the grass of twenty cows'. The schoolmaster, the doctor and the priest are all held in high esteem enjoying a higher rung on the social ladder: 'School is a place for schoolmasters and children', Mena informs Sive.

The tinkers are placed at the lowest stratum of society. Mena repudiates them, as do Thomasheen Seán Rua and Seán Dóta: 'Go on away to yeer smelly caravan and not be disgustin' respectable people'. Conversely, Nanna and Liam Scuab delight in their company: 'God spare you to the roads you travel, Pats ...'

## CUSTOMS AND TRADITIONS

Keane offers us a snapshot of the social mores and customs in Ireland at the time. The rituals of a match are addressed in depth and detail. The cottage kitchen with its evocative symbols of the open hearth, crane, skillet, sugan chairs, milk tank and bags of flour and meal also point towards a more traditional, self-sufficient lifestyle. Everything revolves around the land. Mena handwashes her clothes and makes her own bread while tending to the farm: 'Keep an eye on the bread.

I'm going out to give hay to the cows'. Mike, in the earlier part of the play, is stitching a pony's collar with a shoe-maker's needle.

Rural electrification had not reached all homes in the 1950s. The Glavins used a paraffin lamp and the flame of the open hearth as sources of light. The most popular modes of transport seem to be on foot and the bicycle with the car being the preserve of the school-master, strong farmer and doctor.

Rambling was popular at the time: 'Doing a bit of rambling we are', Thomasheen Seán Rua announces when he calls to visit the Glavins with Seán Dóta. News and general information is dispersed by word of mouth and by the tinkers. This is a gossipy, close-knit community as is seen in the local interest in the scandal of Sive's match to Seán Dóta: 'It is the talk at every cross-roads'. Keane said of that era, 'The rural community was one big family'.

The clay pipe was very popular in the time as is seen from Nanna's addiction to it. The Glavins drink their milk straight from the tank and eat a simple, staple diet: 'The spuds are boiled. I will make a muller of onion dip'.

## FAMILY STRUCTURES

In the mid-twentieth century, it was not unusual for three generations to live in the same house as in the case in *Sive*. This system worked relatively successfully as the older woman helped with the domestic duties of the home and looked after the children while the parents tended to the farm. This does not work well in *Sive* due to the ongoing friction between Nanna and Mena. Mena feels isolated from Nanna and Sive and this created an unpleasant atmosphere in the home: '… the minute I turn my back you're cohackling with that oul boody woman in the corner'. Mike Glavin finds the hatred between his wife and mother intolerable: 'will ye never stop pestering me?'

# THEMES AND ISSUES

## LONELINESS

According to Con Houlihan: 'John B's plays cast a fierce light on the "Hidden Ireland", on a world of poverty and loneliness and sexual frustration'.

Loneliness is a central theme of *Sive*. The forlorn physical setting of the play is sombre and secluded, taking place 'in a remote, mountainy part of southern Ireland'. The farm-land is bad and there is a lot of bogland in the immediate vicinity. The general area does not seem to be densely populated, but there is a mention of Seamas Dónal's cottage at 'the butt of the bohareen'. Notwithstanding, the Glavins seem to be at a far remove from general society: 'I will be going home by the short cut across the mountain', Thomasheen Seán Rua reveals. Allusions to the phuca and the devil are common-place, reinforcing this sense of isolation: 'But think of the dark, girl, and the phuca'.

The play is an exposé of long-suffering human loneliness in rural Ireland in the 1950s. Ironically and unexpectedly, Thomasheen Seán Rua epitomises the despair and anguish of the country bachelor. He regrets not having being able to marry because of his father's suicide and unrelenting poverty. He understands the pain of solitude and elaborates tenderly on living alone: 'I know what it is to be alone in a house when the only word you will hear is a sigh, the sigh of the fire in the hearth dying, with no human words to warm you'. He mourns the absence of physical love and human companionship: 'I know what a man have to do who have no woman to lie with him'. He goes on to confess that he has to turn to alcohol for solace: 'He have to drink hard, or he have to walk under the black sky when every eye is closed to sleep'. Thomasheen Seán Rua hopes the £100 he will earn from the match will secure a match for himself: 'Not so lonesome now! There's a widow woman having a small place beyond the village. £100 would see me settled with her'.

Seán Dóta is another lonely, physically frustrated bachelor in the play: 'How many years have he spent searchin' the country for a young woman?' His desperation for Sive is so great that he is prepared to risk ridicule and scorn to have her. His lust and hunger for physical contact with a woman is evidenced when he makes a vicious pass on Sive on the road and in the lewd, vulgar comments he makes about her on the road. When Pats Bocock remarks on the night before the wedding that it will be a rest for him to marry, he laughs indignantly and asks, 'A rest?' Seán Dóta is sexually obsessed with Sive and this stems from living alone for so many years: ''Tis the flesh of her he do be doting over', Pats Bocock says to Nanna.

Sive also undergoes acute loneliness at the end of the play. Out-witted and over-powered by Mena and Thomasheen Seán Rua, she feels friendless and forsaken. She has been removed by Mena from school, taken away from her Nanna and to crown her misfortunes, she believes Mena's lies that Liam Scuab has more or less turned his back on her. Mena's tactless revelation that she is a 'common bye-child' must have been a grievous blow to her. Abandoned and confused, a shattered Sive takes her own life: 'I saw her running across the bog with only the little frock against the cold of the night. She ran like the wind and she letting cries out of her that would rend your heart. I called after her but she would not stop. She took her own life'.

## LOVE AND MARRIAGE

A hard-headed Mena sees love in practical, business-like, down-to-earth terms. She tells Sive that as a young girl she yearned to escape the poverty trap of her childhood. She claims to have worked tirelessly for her 'fortune' for her match so she could secure the stability and independence of a home of her own: 'We would kill. We would beg, borrow or steal. We would fire embers of fire at the devil to leave the misery of our own house behind us, to make a home with a man, any man that would show four walls to us for his time in the world'.

Romantic love is of no relevance to Mike and Mena Glavin. They are not an amorous couple and they do not openly show affection for each other. They communicate on the harsh, everyday realities of everyday life: 'What have you in the skillet?' When Mike Glavin objects to Sive's proposed match on the grounds that she 'will be dreaming about love with a young man', Thomasheen Seán Rua pokes fun at him and gives a telling account of love in 1950s rural Ireland: 'Love! In the name of God, what do the likes of us know about love? Did he ever give you a little rub behind the ear or run his fingers through your hair and tell you that he would swim the Shannon for you?'

The younger generation in the play find the idea of a match off-putting and repugnant to their ideals about love: 'Liam, would you marry somebody you never saw before?' Sive asks Liam Scuab. Nanna maintains that 'there is a sweet thing to their love'. Their love is gentle, tender and innocent: 'I would marry nobody but you'. Liam Scuab believes this love is worth fighting for and he openly defies Mike Glavin: 'you will not command the lives and happiness of two people who love each other'. We realise how much Sive is in love with Liam Scuab when she is crestfallen after Mena lies to her that he wished her well on her wedding: 'Oh! Liam could never do a thing like that!'

Liam's emotional outburst at Sive's death stems from his heartfelt, consuming love for her: 'The beautiful hair of her! The lovely, silky hair of her!'

# LITERARY GENRE

Critic Fintan O'Toole has said of some of Keane's plays and of *Sive* in particular: 'They're not just melancholic or sad or grim, they are tragic in the full sense, in the Greek sense, in the Shakespearean sense, *Sive* being one of them'. While *Sive* contains some of the motifs of folk-drama, the play has all of the requisite elements to categorically define it as a tragedy. There is the calamitous, catastrophic ending: 'And they laid her for to bury in the clay'. The play is heightened with broad touches of melodrama as occurs in tragedies: 'That the hand of Jesus may strike you dead where you stand'. There is the mounting tension slowly building up to the disastrous ending: 'She's gone, I tell you! The window of the room is open'. The literary concept of the tragic hero is examined in the play through the flawed characters of Thomasheen Seán Rua and Mena. While these two key protagonists are duplicitous and deceitful, they show human vulnerability in climactic moments of the play like the conventional tragic hero of Greek and Shakespearean tragedy: 'I know what it is like in the long hours of the night'.

## HUMOUR

Keane uses humour as a dramatic device to lift the drama out of the depths of despair. The animated exchanges between Nanna and Mena are highly entertaining:

**Mena:** 'Some day that pipe will take fire while you have it hidden and you'll go off in a big, black ball of smoke and ashes'.

**Nanna:** 'If I do,'tis my prayer that the wind will blow me in your direction'.

Thomasheen Seán Rua also relieves the heavy mood of the play with his sharp acerbic witticisms as he mocks Mike Glavin as a would-be lover: 'Did he ever sing the love-songs for you in the far-out part of the night when ye do be alone? He would sooner to stick his snout in a plate of mate and cabbage, or to rub the back of a fattening pig than whisper a bit of his fondness for you'.

## MUSIC AND SONG

Keane uses music and song as a technique to liven and refresh the play through the flamboyant Pats Bocock and Carthalawn. The rhythmic stomping of Pats Bocock's blackthorn stick on the floor, the expressive song of Carthalawn to the striking beat of the bodhrán combine to electrify the dialogue. Their startling, larger than life, lyrics and colourful curses have an arresting impact on audiences: 'May the fleas consume his bed/And the mange eat up his head/That black man from the mountain, Seánín Rua'. At the end of the play, they add to the pathos of Sive's death: 'Oh, come all good men and true, A sad tale I'll tell to you, All of a maiden fair, who died this day.

## LANGUAGE AND IMAGERY

Senator Maurice Hayes said of Keane's language, 'There was the language, the rich torrent of speech, the flashing metaphor and simile, the mixture of Irish and English words, the sense of being between two languages, two cultures'.

The play is rich in exciting, vivacious images. Many of the images are sourced from the world of nature reflecting the close affinity the characters have with their immediate environment: 'There is a black wind coming around the shoulder of the mountain with fangs in it like the tooth of a boar'. There are several references to farm animals, wild animals and fish again displaying the intimate knowledge the characters have of their land and waters: 'You are the bladder of a pig, the snout of a sow; you are the leavings of a hound, the sting of a wasp'.

The language has a poetical, lyrical quality about it. Personification features prominently: 'There's a mad moon in the sky tonight with the stars out of their mind'. The play is teeming with a diverse range of similes: 'The girl is flighty like a colt', 'don't be going around in circles like salmon in a pool'. Metaphors also serve to enhance and accentuate the dialogue: 'The seed is sown; the flower will blossom'. Alliteration injects the language with a musical resonance: 'Snugglin' and sucklin'', 'dodgin' and dartin'', 'dawn till dusk'. Hyperbole figures in the rousing and dramatic imagery: 'Your father a half-starved bocock of a beggar with the Spanish blood galloping through his blood like litters of hungry greyhounds'.

Keane expressly endeavoured to record the natural vernacular of the people of North Kerry. In his life-time, he would jot down snippets from conversations of his neighbours, friends and of customers in his bar. He has stated that the North Kerry dialect was 'the love child of two languages – Elizabethan English and Bardic Irish'. Although the Irish language has not been spoken in the North Kerry area for hundreds of years, there were still distinctive traces of the Gaelic idiom in the North Kerry dialect in the middle of the twentieth century and Keane painstakingly portrays this in the unique and unusual language. Many Irish words and phrases direct from the Gaelic flow naturally and freely into the dialogue, such as, 'bean a' tighe', 'buachall', 'fuastar', 'rann', 'phuca', 'dul amú', 'go mbeirimid beo!' etc. Other words are anglicised derivations from the Irish such as 'doodeen', 'bonham', 'muller'. The Gaelic habit of adding ín to words is evident in words such as 'bohareen', 'wraneen', 'dusteen'. The North Kerry turn of phrase enriches the dialogue: 'Hould your mouth woman', 'A nice bargain you were!', 'She'll be as cracked as the crows …', 'You have great gumption', etc. Keane's language is exceptional and extraordinary in that it is flavoured with its own characteristic North Kerry idiom.

# VISION AND VIEWPOINT

## OPENING – A BLEAK VISION

*Sive* opens with conflict and confrontation between Mena and Nanna Glavin and this contentious atmosphere establishes a gloomy tone for the remainder of the play. While some of the verbal scuffles between these two strong women are comical, their raw hatred for each other does not offer any vision of hope or positivity. There is an ugly, malevolent edge to this strained relationship: 'Fitter for you be having three or four children put from you at this day of your life'.

By throwing Sive, an innocent 'pretty young girl', into this cantankerous mix, Keane shows how goodness and virtue do not stand a chance against aggression and bullying. While Nanna does all she can for Sive, from the outset, her aunt-in-law Mena harasses and wounds her: 'You'll come to no good either, like the one that went before you'.

By kick-starting the play with such naked hostility, Keane is opening the door on a dark, hate-filled world.

## THE VISION AND VIEWPOINT
## OF THE SOCIETY OF THE TIME

The world of 1950s in Ireland contributes significantly to the dark vision of the play. Keane's perception of this society is generally disenchanting and disheartening.

He proves to us how poverty has robbed the society of any moral decency. The gravity of the economic situation at the time forced desperate characters to take desperate measures. Keane uses Mena as a dramatic vehicle to illustrate this viewpoint. Her impoverished background shapes Mena's character, and her moral sense has become less sensitive and her conscience is smothered.

She brutally coerces Sive into the match. Thomasheen Seán Rua also denies his conscience for money when he pushes this improper match on the Glavins and on Sive: 'There will be £100 for me'.

Keane suggests that the repressive Catholic Church helped generate this grim, intolerant society. Suicide and sexuality were taboo subjects in 1950s Ireland due to the restrictive vision of the clergy. The belief that Sive's character was somehow stained or tainted because she was born out of wedlock shows the small-minded viewpoints of a society heavily influenced by the Church. The cold unsympathetic attitude to suicide is addressed at the end of the play when Mike insists that Sive be buried in 'holy ground'.

While the overall mindset of the play is ultimately downbeat and pessimistic, there is evidence that the economic crisis is about to change for the better as is enunciated by Pats Bocock at the end of the play: 'There is money-making everywhere. The face of the country is changing. The small man with the one cow and the pig and the bit of bog is coming into his own'.

## IMAGES AND SYMBOLS

Keane uses many effective symbols and images to portray his own particular vision and viewpoint. Through the repeated references to the devil, Keane's viewpoint reminds us that this is a pernicious world which permits evil to thrive, 'May the devil sweep the hairy creature soon'. The mention of the frightening 'phuca' reiterates this point of view.

The profusion of nature and animal images underlines Keane's assertion that this is a society engrossed with the land to the point of obsession: 'You're like a pet bonham snugglin' and sucklin' for all the good it's doing you'. Likewise, money is a powerful symbol to highlight the greed and avarice of some of the key characters: 'Think of the 200 sovereigns dancing in the heel of your fist'.

# ENDING – VISION AND VIEWPOINT

The play closes on an utterly bleak and tragic note. Nobody emerges triumphant at the end. Sive's suicide destroys the lives of the key characters. Their hopes and expectations are completely dashed.

Mena's dream of getting rid of Nanna and benefiting financially from the match is shattered. Her only legacy will be a lifetime of guilt, blame and accusation as is seen in Liam Scuab's enraged attack on her: 'Go away! … Go away! … You are polluting the pure spirit of the child with your nearness. Go away, witch!' Mike Glavin's conscience will no doubt plague him for a long time to come. Keane goes to great pains to bring home to us that this is a narrow, insular, dismal world and he does this in his portrayal of Mike Glavin's reaction to Sive's death. Mike's fear of the priest and the possible slur on the Glavin name due to death by suicide shows on one level his guilt, but on a more sinister level his terror of the austere Church of the day.

A life of hopelessness and loneliness more than likely awaits Thomasheen Seán Rua and Seán Dóta. The matchmaker will not earn his promised fee and marry his widow-woman and Dóta will not have Sive. Alarmed, they try to absolve themselves of blame by skulking away from the Glavin kitchen: 'Thomasheen edges in to look at the body, then horrified edges slyly away and exits looking around him furtively. He is noticed only by Seán Dóta who follows him as he backs, sneakily to the door. Seán exits'.

The tinkers do not spare anyone at the play's close and are quick to conclude that Sive was murdered. Their haunting lyrics evoke a vision of a dangerous world inhabited by menacing, malicious characters:

> Oh, they murdered lovely Sive,
> She would not be a bride,
> And they laid her dead to bury in the clay.

Audiences, however, are drawn to Nanna at the very end who silently weeps over the corpse of Sive. Her dignified grief underscores the overall vision of loss and melancholy in the play.

# HEROES/VILLAINS

- Keane's unpopular characters are not totally monstrous. They are not the hideous, one-dimensional villains of pantomimes or fairy-tales. Mena and Thomasheen Seán Rua commit serious wrong-doings, especially in the forcing of the match on Sive and in the ill-treatment of Nanna. However, they do earn our sympathy at certain stages of the play. We pity Thomasheen Seán Rua when he speaks about his father's suicide, and the agonising loneliness he feels without a companion. Also, we feel sorry for Mena when Nanna undermines her for being childless and when she talks about her poor childhood.

- Heroism comes in unusual places in *Sive*. The tinkers symbolise goodness and courage in the play. They do not hesitate to speak out against the match in song and they try to enable Sive to elope with Liam Scuab. Nanna also displays fearlessness when she heroically does everything in her power to stop the match.

- Liam Scuab is the embodiment of heroism and nobility in the play. He bravely begs the Glavins to end the match and he does all he can to save Sive from her cruel fate. He is the mouthpiece for Keane at the end of the play when he shows up the dangerous consequences of forced matches.

- Sive is a harmless, inoffensive, girl who represents beauty and innocence in the play.

# RELATIONSHIPS

- The relationship between Nanna and Mena Glavin is vicious. They show nothing but savage contempt for each other. Mena is jealous of Nanna's closeness to Sive. She constantly complains about her pipe-smoking. Nanna returns Mena's insults with hurtful remarks about Mena's childlessness. This abominable mother-in-law/daughter relationship creates a nasty atmosphere in the Glavin home.
- In contrast, Liam Scuab's relationship with Sive is warm, loving and gentle. Likewise, Nanna and Sive are very affectionate towards each other. Nanna and the tinkers show great regard for each other.

# GLOSSARY

Achree: darling/love [from Gaelic: *a chroí*]

Aisy: easy

Amadawn: fool/idiot [from Gaelic *amadán*]

Bane of cows: large amount of cows [colloquial]

Bean a' tighe: woman of the house [from Gaelic]

Bell-rag: humiliate, embarrass [colloquial]

Blather: foolish talk/nonsense

Bocock: beggar [from Gaelic *bacach*]

Bodhrán: type of tambourine made from goat-skin

Bohareen: short narrow road [from Gaelic *bóithrín*]

Bonham: piglet [from Gaelic: *banbh*]

Bornack: barnacle [from Gaelic: *bairneach*]

Bostoon: foolish person [from Gaelic: *bostún*]

Brace: mechanism that holds parts together or in place

Buachall: boy [from Gaelic]

Bualam ski: nonsense

Bye-child: derogatory term to describe a child born out of wedlock; secondary child, less important, inferior [colloquial]

Canavaun: white fluffy cotton which grows in bog [from Gaelic: *ceann-abhán*]

Clane: clean

Cnabshealing: complaining [from Gaelic: *ag cnáimhseáil*]

Cohackling: scheming/colluding [colloquial]

Coif: swept back hair with wave in front

Consumptive: disease which destroys part of the body, especially the lungs [tuberculosis]

County Home: Poor House

Cracked: colloquial expression for giddy/wild

Crane: a swinging metal arm in a fireplace, used to hold a kettle or pot over the fire

Craw: stomach of an animal

Cumar: ravine, usually with stream [from Gaelic: *cumar*]

Curam: charge, responsibility [from Gaelic: *cúram*]

Curran-y cake: cake made with currants in it [colloquial]

Dacent: decent

Diggle: colloquial for devil

Doodeen: a short-stemmed clay pipe [from Gaelic: *dúidín*]

Dorn: a handful, fist [from Gaelic: *dorn*]

Dul amú: to go astray, here means idiot [from Gaelic: *dul amú*]

Eejit: an idiot, fool [colloquial]

Faix: faiths [colloquial]

Faldals: bits and pieces

Folly: follow

Fortune: dowry

Fuastar: fuss, activity, rush, hurry [from Gaelic: *fuadar*]

Gad: colloquial suggests hatred tinkers have for Thomasheen

Gainsay: deny, contradict or dispute

Gall: boldness, impudence, nerve

Gibble: rag [from Gaelic: *giobal*]

Gleann na nGealt: Glen of the Lunatics [between Tralee and Dingle, Co. Kerry]

Go mbeirimid beo: may we be alive together again

Gob: mouth/bird's beak [from Gaelic]

Gomaill/Gomeril: vexation, annoying, foolish

Gorsoon: boy [from Gaelic: *garsún*]

Gradhbhar: generous, affectionate, amiable [from Gaelic: *grádhbhar*]

Grain o' tea: a small amount [colloquial]

Gumption: cheek/nerve

Hardy thief: robber but colloquial for strong, stubborn

Hearth: near the floor of the fireplace and surrounding area. It is symbolic of the house and home.

Huist: Silence/stop/quiet [from Gaelic]

I've come to the last sod: I have come to the end of the road with you, I have finished with you [colloquial]

Jinnet: a cross between a donkey and a pony

Ketching: catching

Leanav: child [from the Gaelic: *leanbh*]

Lurgadawn: thin-skinned, lazy useless person [from Gaelic: *lorgadán*]

Mate: meat

Milch: milk cow

Moll the Wag: gossipy woman [colloquial]

Moryeah: as if [from Gaelic: *mar dhea*]

Muller: saucepan

Nate: neat

Oinseach: foolish woman [from Gaelic: *óinseach*]

Pauperised: very poor person

Petticoat: a skirt worn beneath the dress or outer skirt worn by women or girls

Phuca: hobgoblin, sprite, ghost [from Gaelic: *púca*]

Pot: chamber pot [sign of wealth]

Pratey: colloquial expression for potato [from Gaelic: *práta*]

Prattle: careless talk

Puss: frown, sad face [colloquial]

Rameish: nonsensical talk/rigmarole [from Gaelic: *ráiméis*]

Rann: verse [from Gaelic: *rann*]

Sciath: semi-circular basket made from twigs, container

Scythe: a long, curved blade on a long handle

Skewer: pin for holding meat together. Here it means 'bad luck' [colloquial]

Skillet: a saucepan with a long handle

Smohawnach: large/great/prolonged [from Gaelic]

Sugan chairs: a wooden kitchen chair, with a hand woven straw seat

Tamaill: a while [from Gaelic: *tamall*]

Tathaire: hangar-on, cheeky person, scrounger [from Gaelic]

Tay: tea [Gaelic pronunciation]

Tetter: itching skin diseases, such as eczema or psoriasis

To own them: to acknowledge/befriend them [colloquial]

Wraneen: small brown bird

# Song from

# Sive

Oh! Mike Glav - in you're the man; You was al - ways in the van; With a dacent house to old man and gor — soon, May white snuff be at your wake, Baker's bread and curran'y cake, And plinty on your table late and soon ———

Transcribed by Oonagh Connon